GREEN HELL CURSE KILLS
MAN IN N.Y.

Explorer Stricken in Doc Savage's Office
Thousands of Miles from Matto Grosso

The newspapers were having a field day at the expense of THE MAN OF BRONZE. Lurid accounts abounded. The victim, it appeared, had gone to Doc Savage's office for advice, but had been dropped by the green death before he could tell his story. There was no mention anywhere of the second visitor to THE MAN OF BRONZE. Doc hadn't seen fit to mention that to the police!

Doc Savage is up to his massive neck in jungle mystery!

THE GREEN DEATH

D1450856

THE MAN OF BRONZE
THE THOUSAND-HEADED MAN
METEOR MENACE
THE POLAR TREASURE
BRAND OF THE WEREWOLF
THE LOST OASIS
THE MONSTERS
THE LAND OF TERROR
THE MYSTIC MULLAH
THE PHANTOM CITY
FEAR CAY
QUEST OF QUI
LAND OF ALWAYS-NIGHT
THE FANTASTIC ISLAND
MURDER MELODY
THE SPOOK LEGION
THE RED SKULL
THE SARGASSO OGRE
PIRATE OF THE PACIFIC
THE SECRET IN THE SKY
COLD DEATH
THE CZAR OF FEAR
FORTRESS OF SOLITUDE
THE GREEN EAGLE
THE DEVIL'S PLAYGROUND
DEATH IN SILVER
THE MYSTERY UNDER
  THE SEA
THE DEADLY DWARF
THE OTHER WORLD
THE FLAMING FALCONS
THE ANNIHILIST
THE SQUEAKING GOBLINS
MAD EYES
THE TERROR IN THE NAVY

DUST OF DEATH
RESURRECTION DAY
HEX
RED SNOW
WORLD'S FAIR GOBLIN
THE DAGGER IN THE SKY
MERCHANTS OF DISASTER
THE GOLD OGRE
THE MAN WHO SHOOK THE
  EARTH
THE SEA MAGICIAN
THE MEN WHO SMILED NO
  MORE
THE MIDAS MAN
LAND OF LONG JUJU
THE FEATHERED OCTOPUS
THE SEA ANGEL
DEVIL ON THE MOON
HAUNTED OCEAN
THE VANISHER
THE MENTAL WIZARD
HE COULD STOP THE
  WORLD
THE GOLDEN PERIL
THE GIGGLING GHOSTS
POISON ISLAND
THE MUNITIONS MASTER
THE YELLOW CLOUD
THE MAJII
THE LIVING FIRE MENACE
THE PIRATE'S GHOST
THE SUBMARINE
  MYSTERY
THE MOTION MENACE
THE GREEN DEATH

THE
GREEN DEATH

A DOC SAVAGE ADVENTURE

BY KENNETH ROBESON

A NATIONAL GENERAL COMPANY

THE GREEN DEATH

A Bantam Book / published by arrangement with
The Condé Nast Publications Inc.

PRINTING HISTORY

Originally published in DOC SAVAGE *Magazine November 1938*
Bantam edition published November 1971

Bantam Books are published by Bantam Books, Inc., a National
General company. Its trade-mark, consisting of the words "Bantam
Books" and the portrayal of a bantam, is registered in the United
States Patent Office and in other countries. Marca Registrada.
Bantam Books, Inc., 666 Fifth Avenue, New York, N.Y. 10019.

PRINTED IN THE UNITED STATES OF AMERICA

CONTENTS

Chapter I

JUNGLE DOOM

DEATH was abroad in the jungle. The moist hot air was ominous, as the sun beat in vain on matted trees and vines, unable to pierce the gloom beneath.

Through that gloom a man raced.

He was a very tall, very thin man, with a peculiar sallow complexion that now was literally streaming with perspiration. His eyes, behind the glasses he wore, were worried. Occasionally he would dart a quick glance over his shoulder, then he would plunge on, even though he knew escape was impossible.

The attack had come just at dawn. All the natives who had made up his party had either been killed or had fled, panic-stricken, in that first attack.

There had been soft *puft* sounds, and death had arrived in the form of poisoned arrows.

The tall, thin man had snatched a gun and fired recklessly toward the foes he could not see; then he, too, had run. There had been nothing else to do.

That had been hours ago. The sun was high now. And hour after hour he had kept up a steady jogging pace, never seeming to tire. But he had not shaken off pursuit. Only minutes ago a single poisoned arrow had sped past his head. He had seen nothing, heard nothing; but death was trailing him.

Despite the worry in his eyes, the tall man did not appear afraid; rather, he seemed irritated, as if he had been interrupted while performing an important task. Suddenly, he paused. A shot had sounded from ahead.

A peculiar, almost unbelieving look came to the man's eyes. That shot would indicate that other white men were near—and that was impossible. He was hundreds of miles

1

from the closest village. There could be no help, yet there had been a shot.

He increased his speed quickly, running easily, winding and twisting through the big trees, dodging underbrush, racing through wild country that never before had been explored. A gun was in the holster at his hip, but he ignored that. Only two shots were left in that gun. And two shots could mean nothing, when he never had been given even a glimpse of those who pursued him.

Then the tall man's speed slowed. His face became puzzled and questioning, nostrils twitching uneasily. Premonition of danger, of unseen, terrible danger, made the short hairs rise on his neck, sent icy thrills down his spine despite the heat.

All sound had ceased. The jungle was still—a strange, frightening stillness. Not a bird stirred; not a monkey chattered in the trees.

THE heavy, moisture-laden air carried a faint odor, an unusual, though not unpleasant odor such as might have been caused by a field of flowers. But there were no flowers.

Only for a moment did the tall, thin man hesitate. Then his pale lips tightened. Unconsciously he freed the gun in its holster. His nerves were tighter than ever before. Ever since dawn he had run with the feeling that unseen eyes were staring at his back; that every move he made was being watched.

That feeling was gone now. It was as if those who pursued him had quit the chase, had fallen back from a danger far more vivid and real than any their intended victim might prepare for them. The very absence of that feeling of being watched made peril more real.

Sunlight suddenly flashed ahead, blinding in its brilliance after the gloom of the jungle. There was a cleared area directly in front. The cleared area was semicircular in shape. Beyond it were more trees, then high cliffs.

An unbelieving gasp came from the thin man. His eyes were wide behind the glasses he wore. A strange sight presented itself to him on those cliffs, a sight that seemed unreal, as if he were visioning a scene from some bygone age.

Long legs pounding, he burst from the jungle, started

across the cleared area toward that scene. For just an instant he felt strong, able to conquer anything he might meet. Then an expression almost of terror swept over his features.

He knew he was lost; knew that he had left one danger only to encounter another, one that he could not defeat. Fiercely he turned, tried to run back toward the comparative safety of the jungle. His knees buckled under him, and a thin cry came from his lips.

Then he was very still; breathing stopped.

His body was twisted and contorted horribly. The skin no longer was sallow. It was green, a startling shade of green. He appeared to have been mummified, as if he had been dead for many years.

Chapter II

THE CURSE FULFILLED

THE story first broke when three men staggered out of the jungle. The world was thrilled, horrified and more than a little unbelieving. The men's clothing was in tatters. Their faces and bodies were swollen and red from numerous insect bites. They were hungry, almost starving, their ribs showing plainly. Their eyes were wide and staring. Fear was written there, as well as suffering from the hardships they had undergone.

Kind-hearted officials gave them food, fresh clothing and medical attention. And bit by bit the story came out.

One, who said he was Hugo Parks, acted as spokesman. Parks was a small man, with a body now more thin than ever. But his head was huge; it dwarfed the rest of his body, gave him a peculiar appearance. It was easy to understand why his companions called him "Brains."

These three, Parks said, were the sole survivors of a party of twenty. They had entered Brazil from Paraguay, he insisted, and had made their way to the dread Matto Grosso section of Brazil, the "Green Hell" section.

Parks said they were explorers. Whatever the authorities thought, they kept to themselves.

After weeks of struggling, Parks recounted, they penetrated the Green Hell section farther than any other white men had ever gone.

And they had found a fabulous, lost city!

Newspapers grabbed onto the story. It had the element of mystery they liked. And, from their files, they told again of other explorers who had attempted to penetrate the district and whose fate never had been definitely learned.

There was Colonel P. H. Fawcett, the noted British explorer, who, with his son, Jack, and a companion, had vanished in 1925. They, too, had entered the wild Matto Grosso

4

jungle. They had been searching for a mythical "Atlantis," a lost city and a lost race. They had never been seen alive again. Some reports said they had been killed by hostile Indians.

Then there was Paul Redfern, the American flier, also believed lost in the same district. More recently, one year before, another American flier, "Scotty" Falcorn, had also disappeared in the Matto Grosso jungle. He had been hunting for Redfern.

The lost city was there, Hugo Parks said. It was inhabited by a mysterious tribe of white Indians. And it was guarded by a strange, horrible green death—a death that left the victim mummified, contorted in agony!

BLASTS of publicity filled the newspapers. Almost fabulous offers for first-person accounts of their experiences were cabled the three survivors.

They appeared strangely indifferent, almost suspiciously so, the Brazilian authorities thought. For there were a couple of minor items the newspapers did not get.

One was that Parks carried a small, lead box. He refused to let anyone see what was in this box, except that he took oath it was not treasure of any kind.

Another detail was a small bundle that another of the men carried. Upon examination, this proved to contain only a part of a letter, a belt buckle and a watch. Parks refused to explain what this meant.

The third point was not so mysterious, but it was unusual. The day after their arrival from the jungle, a New York bank cabled a letter of credit in Parks's name. It came even before their story had reached the outside world. It was for a very large sum of money.

After their first stories, the three men became uncommunicative. It seemed they did not want to answer questions of any kind. They appeared more fearful than ever before. They hardly were civil to those who had befriended them. They were pressed for explanations. And just before they left for the United States, Parks sprung his bombshell.

They had been warned, he said mysteriously, to do as little talking as possible. There was more to the lost city than they had told. Savages had whispered a warning. A curse would follow them. No matter how far or how fast they fled, death was to catch up with them. Parks shuddered as he spoke of that menace.

It was the green death!

That was the part the world did not believe. In fact, some newspapers, angry because offers for more details had been snubbed, hinted almost openly that the men were impostors, expressed doubt that they had ever reached the Green Hell section.

Experienced jungle men in Brazil expressed no such doubts. The men knew too much about the country they said they had visited. No one could know all they did without actually having been where they said they were.

But it was while the publicity was dying down that the men vanished. They rented a private plane and disappeared. A week later they passed through the customs at Miami. And the storm of newspaper comment broke out in redoubled form.

For now it was learned that Parks was carrying the small lead box. And the customs men insisted that this box be opened before Parks was permitted to enter the country with it.

The huge-headed man submitted with bad grace. Afterwards, the customs men wondered why. There was no need for such secrecy. The box was empty. At least, the customs officials found nothing in it.

A DAY later the men were in New York City. Newspaper headlines read:

TRIO FLEEING DREAD CURSE
OF GREEN DEATH

The tenor of the stories was more than half-humorous. The three returning explorers had been openly hostile to newspapermen, had refused to answer questions, and had eluded reporters as swiftly as possible. The newspapermen were paying them back.

The more serious-minded publications referred to the reputed curse of King Tut's tomb, which was supposed to have claimed the life of many connected with its discovery and opening. Scientific writers pointed out that there could be no basis in fact for such beliefs, but that they had long been cherished, and that fear often killed when there was no other known cause.

The tabloids kidded the whole thing, deciding now that these men probably had been raving when they first came out of the jungle, suffering from privation, and had told stories they knew would not stand expert scrutiny, so were taking refuge in silence.

No answer came from Parks and his two companions. They sought and found a hideaway. But they prepared to call at once upon Doc Savage.

The biggest one of the trio was selected to go. He was tall and thick-chested. His eyes were colorless, showing no emotion whatever. Parks called him "Frick."

Frick powdered features that were deeply tanned from the tropics. It made him appear pale. That was the only disguise he used. Then he drifted into the street, worked his way toward the towering skyscraper where Doc Savage had his offices.

He didn't have to ask directions—he had been in New York before. And everyone who had ever visited the city had heard of Doc Savage.

At a bookstore, Frick paused. A new volume was on display. It was being strongly advertised.

"ATOMIC RESEARCH SIMPLIFIED," read the title. "By Clark Savage, Jr."

Beside a pile of books was a big sign. It read:

READ THE LATEST WORK OF CLARK SAVAGE, JR.
THE WORLD'S MOST FAMOUS SCIENTIST,
EXPLORER AND ADVENTURER.

Frick's pale, colorless eyes did not change; but his mouth worked curiously. It was well known that Doc Savage was a famous scientist. He understood medicine, hydrodynamics and meteorology equally well. With his five aids, each an expert in a separate line, Doc had long been recognized throughout the world as one of the most fearless foes of crime.

Frick turned a corner, approached a huge skyscraper.

Then he halted suddenly, one hand clutched at his heart. A strange expression flashed over his features, an expression in which wonderment was mingled with fear.

ONLY for a moment did Frick hesitate. Then his husky form jerked erect, his breathing became more normal. He sped into the office building.

"Eighty-sixth floor, and make it snappy!" he snarled at an elevator operator.

The operator looked at him curiously, then shrugged. He was accustomed to having strange-appearing men rush in and demand to be taken immediately to the floor where Doc Savage had his offices.

As the door clanged open on the eighty-sixth floor, Frick appeared to be swaying. With difficulty, he forced his way out into the corridor. His footsteps were uncertain as he moved slowly down until he reached a door that bore the sign: "CLARK SAVAGE, JR."

There was no sign of a knob or bell on the door. Frick's colorless eyes half closed. He slumped against the door.

An instant later, and he pulled himself erect. A man stood before him. Photo-electric cells had given warning of Frick's approach; had opened the door.

The man who stood there did not appear big. It was only when Frick pulled up that he realized the other was even larger than he, but so perfectly put together that it was not apparent.

His features were bronze-colored; his hair, tight against his skull, was only a slightly lighter shade. There was no expression on his face, but his eyes held Frick's attention. They were strangely compelling eyes. Gold flakes seemed to whirl in their depths.

"I—I seem to feel faint," Frick gulped. He slumped, tried again to straighten. His features changed. Stark terror showed in every line. Again his hand clutched at his heart.

"It's got——" His shriek broke off in mid-breath. He dropped to the floor.

A low, trilling sound seemed to fill the corridor. It seemed to come from everywhere, yet from no particular spot. It was an unconscious sound Doc Savage made when he was surprised.

His visitor was very dead. An expression of ghastly pain and horror was frozen on his features. Those features no longer were pale. They were green. The man's entire body was green and queerly contorted. The body itself was as stiff as it had been petrified.

The strange curse of the Matto Grosso had been fulfilled, thousands of miles away.

The Great Devil's...

"Watch there, you hairy mile of the stone age," a voice round behind him...

"Monk," lips moved again. He was calmer proud of his...

Chapter III

A RAID

THE bronze man's low, trilling sound had been heard. There were other sounds from inside the office. They were strange noises.

First there was a queer squealing, grunting noise. Then came a chattering and whining. A moment later came action. Two very peculiar objects raced into view, almost colliding with Doc.

The one in the lead might have been called a pig, but it was probably the homeliest pig outside a "believe-it-or-not" exhibition. It had a very long snout, big ears and a skinny, hard body. Its extra thin legs were carrying it along very fast.

Behind it trailed what undoubtedly was an ape of some type. It had exceptionally long arms, hanging well below its knees and tiny eyes showed in a face covered with fur. Right now it appeared to be somewhat angry.

"Give me that banana, you long-eared porcine monstrosity, or I'll tear you pork chop from pork chop," came a bellow, apparently from the ape.

"You can't have it! You can't have it!" a voice squealed. The voice seemingly came from the pig.

There was a long banana tied firmly on the pig's back. The ape stretched out one long arm for it, missed, and redoubled its speed.

Roars of laughter came from inside the office. Another figure appeared, one that strongly resembled the ape. The man was bigger about the middle, and there was no hair on his face, but those were the only radical differences in appearance. His tiny eyes were set in deep pits of gristle. His arms hung well below the knees.

Now his lips were moving noiselessly, and his face was creased with what he fondly hoped was a smile. More words came from the running pig and ape.

10

"Stop it, Monk, you hairy relic of the stone age!" a voice roared behind him.

"Monk's" lips moved again. He was quite proud of his gift of ventriloquism. It was he who was making the animals appear to talk.

Then Monk, formally known as Lieutenant Colonel Andrew Blodgett Mayfair, one of the best chemists in the world, brought his two hundred and sixty pounds to a sudden halt. He had seen Doc—and the figure Doc was bending over.

"Ham!" he called. His voice was thin and piping, in strange contrast to his big frame.

There was movement behind him. "Ham's" slender, immaculately dressed form came forward swiftly. Monk and Ham delighted in rough jests; in fact, the pets were part of their idea of humor, but Ham knew when Monk had stopped playing.

A thin whistle came from Ham. His face sobered, his eyes flashed shrewdly. As Brigadier General Theodore Marley Brooks, Ham was known to have one of the keenest legal minds in the country.

Down the hall, Chemistry, the ape, had overtaken Habeas Corpus, the pig. He was holding the pig almost lovingly under one arm, while with the other hairy fist he plucked the banana from Habeas's back, ate it with every indication of enjoyment.

None of the three behind them noticed. Monk's tiny eyes were glowing. "Trouble? Any chance of a fight?" he asked Doc. Even more than kidding Ham, the hairy chemist loved to battle.

Doc did not reply in words. He merely moved aside so the others could see the form of the fallen man clearly.

"One of the three from Matto Grosso!" Ham gasped. His eyes widened. "And Johnny is down in that district somewhere!"

Doc Savage came erect. His eyes, like twin pools of revolving gold flakes, were impossible to read. His bronze features were without expression.

"Bring the body inside," he said quietly.

Monk grunted, heaved the mummified body up easily, carried it inside the office. Chemistry grunted also. He lifted Habeas Corpus in as near as imitation of Monk's actions as he could, and followed the chemist.

"But Johnny——" Ham repeated.

"Still no response from him," a new voice broke in. The speaker was a mountain of a man, full six feet four inches tall. His face was severe, the mouth thin and grim, the features as a whole bearing a puritanical look. His arms were enormous, his fists bony monstrosities. An open door behind him showed a compact radio room, with many strange devices about the walls.

"You have tried every test again, Renny?" Doc Savage asked.

The giant nodded. "Renny," more properly known as Colonel John Renwick, an internationally-known engineer, appeared worried.

"I tried him on the wave length of our own microwave set," he said slowly. "Then I thought he might be receiving, but be unable to send, so I tried the ray vibrator. I got no response from that, either."

Doc's gold-flecked eyes flashed slightly. The ray vibrator was an invention of his own, one through which he sometimes kept in touch with his men when radio transmission would not work. If Johnny had heard Renny's calls, he would have hooked up a small, oscillating tube. The resultant waves could easily be picked up on the sensitive devices in the radio room.

"That makes three weeks now," Monk put in. The others said nothing. Comment was superfluous.

"Johnny," William Harper Littlejohn to students of geology and archaeology the world over, was on a trip of his own. He had been anxious to investigate some of the remarkable reports he had heard of the Matto Grosso region. And his first radio messages had indicated his hopes of finding new things had been realized.

Then those radio messages had stopped. Something must be wrong. Something *had* to be wrong.

"If we only knew just where——" Ham started. Then he frowned.

Doc inclined his head, but said nothing. Renny noticed

the body where Monk had put it in an adjoining room. He started, then his stern face paled slightly.

"The green death of the Matto Grosso," Renny muttered. "Do you suppose Johnny——" He choked.

"First, we will see if we can learn what the green death is," Doc Savage said. His calm voice brought sudden confidence to his men. Johnny undoubtedly was in a spot of some kind or other, but these men of his had an almost unbelievable reliance in the bronze man. They had seen him in action.

Doc wheeled the body back farther into his suite of offices. The room where he halted was as complete an operating room as could be found in most modern hospitals.

Renny watched interestedly. He expected to see Doc perform an autopsy. Instead, the bronze man's actions were strange.

First, he took a long tube from a cabinet. The tube was horn-shaped at one end. The other end vanished in a vacuum-appearing box. There was a bellows arrangement at one side.

Doc placed this over the body, worked the bellows. Once more, his trilling sound came, faint but penetrating. An indicator moved on top of the vacuum-like box.

"What the——" began Renny. Then he paused.

Doc was removing the man's shirt. His gold-flecked eyes were glinting strangely.

A bellow came from Renny. Doc Savage whirled. A door leading into the hall had opened slightly; a man's face was peering through.

The man gave a startled bleat. He turned, tried to run. He had no chance. The next instant Renny had yanked the door open. One of his bony monstrosities of a fist popped out, caught the other by the collar.

As easily as if the man had been weightless, Renny yanked him back into the room.

THE man was of medium height, with black hair that looked as if it had been bleached by tropical heat. He was trembling as though suffering a chill from malaria.

But his eyes were focused hard on the green body of the dead man.

"Frick!" he gasped. His voice was a mixture of awe and fear. "It—it really got him!"

"You know him? You another of those three guys who came out of the Matto Grosso jungle?" Renny demanded. His lips were set in thin, puritanical lines.

The man nodded without speaking.

"Bring him into the main office," Doc said quietly.

The man seemed more than willing to get away from the sight of the body, for he almost ran ahead of Renny. Doc followed more slowly.

"Now if you will explain?" Doc prompted.

Renny stood with his big fists planted on his hips. He looked very tough. Monk and Ham gathered about curiously. Even Chemistry and Habeas Corpus stopped their romping.

The man gulped; when he spoke, his voice was thick, his words hardly understandable.

"I—I'm afraid," he muttered. "It—it got Frick! It'll get me."

"Nothing will get you while you are here. Tell us what you fear. Possibly we can help you," Doc Savage said.

"There were three of us. Now there are two," the man said weakly.

"Yes?"

With an effort, the other pulled himself together. His trembling quieted. "My name is Thorne," he said. "With Frick, the one who's dead in there, and Hugo Parks, I was one of the three who escaped the Brazilian jungle alive. You have read our story in the newspapers. Part of it wasn't believed. But we knew it was true, knew a curse would follow us. We knew we needed your help. That is why Frick came here. That is why I followed."

Doc nodded. He did not speak.

Thorne wet his lips, his fists clenched. "We saw fantastic things in that jungle, Mr. Savage. We went in there looking for gold. You have heard—everyone has heard—of the fabled treasure of the Incas, supposed to be hidden in the Green Hell district. We didn't find it. But we did find——" His voice trailed off. Once again his face paled.

"You found what?" Renny demanded harshly.

"Death—horrible death!" Thorne's voice was scarcely a

whisper. "The green death!" His eyes became wide and staring; his trembling was uncontrolled.

Doc Savage stepped forward, caught the other by the shoulder and shook him hard. Sanity returned to the man's eyes.

"We found a city of unspeakable beauty," the man grated. "People live there, but no one can enter. It is guarded by this green death. Y-you will start to approach and you will suddenly fall. Your body turns green and mummified—just as Frick's did. Medicine men of other tribes told us that death would follow us. It has."

The man paused, shuddered. His voice rose shrilly. "We saw another white man die, too. He was not of our party. And when we went to look for his body, it was gone. But I'll prove to you——" He halted dramatically, reached inside the shirt he wore. Then he froze.

A woman's scream sounded in the corridor outside. At the same moment lights flashed on a panel, there was the muted sound of an alarm bell.

Monk and Ham acted as one person. Without hesitation, they leaped toward the door that led into the corridor. They did not touch either knob or button, but the door opened before them. Photoelectric cells took care of that.

Renny dived toward the operating room where Frick's body had been left. Renny was fast; he moved like a ten-second man. Yet before the big engineer reached the first door, a bronze shadow flitted past him.

Doc Savage's speed was deceptive. Even when he was traveling swiftest, he did not appear to be exerting himself, so smoothly did his muscles work.

Blam! Blam!

Two shots sounded sharply from the corridor. There were startled exclamations from Monk and Ham. They skidded to a halt right at the door, leaned out carefully. Then Monk bellowed shrilly and pounded outside, Ham at his heels.

The man who called himself Thorne grinned peculiarly. Strangely, all fear seemed to leave him suddenly. His movements were calm and deliberate. Neither Doc nor his aids noticed him. Doc already had reached the operating room. A moment later Renny pounded in.

The bronze man halted, his face expressionless as always, but his flake-gold eyes narrowed slightly. Renny's severe expression relaxed a trifle. The body was still on the operating table. Nothing appeared disturbed.

"But the alarm sounded. I know somebody must have tried to get in here," the engineer argued.

"The shirt," Doc said quietly.

"Holy cow!" Renny's jaw dropped. The shirt Doc had removed from Frick was gone.

Footsteps pounded loudly in the corridor outside. Soon they returned. Monk entered the room, his homely face a picture of dejection. Ham didn't appear his usual dapper self, either.

"She got away," Monk said glumly.

"She?" Renny exclaimed.

"That accounts for Monk's disappointment," Ham put in slyly. "But naturally, any girl who ever got a look at a face like his would beat it."

Doc glanced at both of them swiftly. Ham dropped his bantering pose.

"We only got a glimpse," he said ruefully. "Somebody fired a couple of slugs, and that slowed us up. When we did get out, we caught just a flash of this girl ducking down the stairs at the end of the hall. We followed, but there are two dozen offices she could have slipped into. She was gone."

"I saw her face," Monk put in.

Ham opened his mouth for a good-natured crack, then clamped his lips back together. There were times when Monk really didn't care to be kidded.

"I've seen that face before. I'll know how to locate that girl," the homely chemist went on grimly.

"And meantime, the shirt is gone," Renny said harshly. "I don't know what Doc wanted with it, but he thought it was important. So it must have been."

The three looked at Doc. He said nothing. Instead, he turned back to the office where they had been talking with Thorne.

The office was empty now. Only Doc did not appear surprised.

Then a startled exclamation came from Ham. His gaze

was riveted on several objects lying on a table. There was a wrist watch, a belt buckle and part of a letter.

"He said he had proof to show that another white man had died," Ham breathed. "And these——"

"Are Johnny's," Doc concluded.

For a moment, all four were silent. Their worst fears were realized. Likable Johnny, the big-worded anthropologist, was dead, killed by the mysterious green horror.

"There might be some mistake," Monk said, but there was no hope in his voice.

"We can at least find out for sure," Doc Savage said softly.

Chapter IV

MONK FINDS TROUBLE

THE newspapers had a field day. Ham paid three cents for an afternoon edition and made a face as he saw the headlines:

GREEN HELL CURSE KILLS MAN IN N. Y.

EXPLORER STRICKEN IN DOC SAVAGE'S OFFICE, THOUSANDS OF MILES FROM MATTO GROSSO

A lurid account followed. The victim, it appeared, had gone to Doc Savage's office for advice, but had been dropped by the green death before he could tell his story. There was no mention of the bronze man's second visitor. Doc hadn't seen fit to mention that to the police.

Monk scowled, looked again at the picture he carried.

The picture was from an advertisement in a popular magazine. A young woman was shown in the briefest of white bathing suits. She had an excellent figure, one that usually would have more than held the hairy chemist's pleased attention. But now he appeared far from pleased.

"Daggonit!" he muttered. "How many more places do we have to go before we get results?"

Ham grinned. "First time I ever heard you complain when you were on the trail of a pretty girl," he gibed.

Monk's scowl deepened. "And why does a pretty one like her have to be mixed up in this?" he growled. "Where does she fit in, anyway?"

"She was just using a novel approach to gain your interest," Ham assured him blandly.

Monk didn't even dignify that one with a reply. His feet were tired. Already, it seemed to him, they had walked a thousand miles on hot New York pavements.

18

As Ham swung a cane nonchalantly, Monk consulted an address book and paused. Then he entered an office building, Ham at his heels. They took an elevator to the third floor and walked to an office bearing the sign: "MEREDITH'S MODEL AGENCY."

As he reached for the knob, the door swung open and a man rushed out, almost knocking the chemist off his feet. One of Monk's big paws shot out, grabbed the other by the shoulder.

"Watch where you're goin', guy!" he piped.

The other swore. One hand darted up toward his armpit and his hard face contorted into a snarl.

A surprised look flashed across Monk's face, then he grinned. His right fist came up, hard. But it didn't connect.

Ham caught his arm, yanked him back. In the same instant the other lunged and broke free. His hand dropped to his side and he almost ran toward the elevator.

"Daggonit, Ham," Monk shrilled excitedly, "that guy tried to pull a gun on me? Let me get him! Let me——"

He was still sputtering as Ham propelled him on into the office of Meredith's Model Agency. The dapper lawyer pulled the advertisement from Monk's hand, dropped it on the desk in front of a good-looking girl.

"This model listed with your agency?" Ham asked pleasantly. He swung his sword cane with an air of detached boredom.

The girl's eyes widened slightly. "W-why yes," she said. "That's Gloria Delpane."

Monk suddenly regained his good humor. "Where does she live? How can we get in touch with her?" he asked swiftly.

Ham grinned, dropped a ten-dollar bill on the table. "Here is the agency's fee. We prefer to call on her, to make sure she is the type we desire," he explained smoothly.

The address was given promptly. "But you may have to wait," the girl warned. "Another man was here only a moment ago. He also was asking for Miss Delpane's address. She certainly is getting popular, and——"

The girl broke off. She no longer had an audience.

Monk and Ham didn't wait for an elevator. They dived down the stairs three steps at a time, rushed for a cab.

They were in such a hurry they didn't see the hard-faced man waiting across the street. The man smiled oddly, went into a cigar store and used the telephone.

As Ham often pointed out, Monk did have an eye for the girls. The hairy chemist had got only one look at the girl running from Doc's office, but that had been enough. He knew he had seen her before. It took him some time to remember where, however; but when he did, he soon found a magazine containing an ad for which she had posed. The round of model agencies had followed.

Neither Monk nor Ham had any idea why the hard-faced man also wanted to find the girl. But they did know that something was screwy. The hard-faced one was tough. That had been apparent when he'd started to go for his gun.

What connection all of this could have with the green death, or Johnny, or why anyone in New York should be taking such an interest in the affair, was more than either could figure out.

But the girl had got the shirt. Doc wanted it. That was enough for Monk and Ham.

Doc and Renny also were busy. Their actions were odd.

Each wore peculiar type glasses. The glasses were almost goggles, with queer-colored lenses and sidepieces that fitted close against the face, keeping out all light.

They walked with their heads down, while pedestrians stepped aside to give them room. First, they left the big office building; then, they went down the sidewalk to a subway kiosk.

"Holy cow!" Renny muttered disgustedly.

Doc said nothing as they entered the underground station and took an uptown local. At every stop they got off, walked up and down the platform, then took another train.

New Yorkers, accustomed to eccentric sights, paid little attention. But two men did. They might have been brothers of the hard-faced man Monk and Ham had encountered. At least, they had the same expression, and their armpits bulged suspiciously. They trailed Renny and the bronze man.

Doc did not appear to notice the two.

Through the glasses, faint, luminous marks were visible. They were marks left by the shoes Thorne wore. Doc had seated his visitor at a spot in his office where the shoes came in contact with a preparation, invisible to the naked eye, but clearly seen through the queer glasses.

This made it possible to trail Thorne, although use of the subway complicated matters. It was necessary to check each stop, to determine at which the other had left the train. Finding Thorne was important. It was vital to know just where in the Matto Grosso he had seen Johnny killed.

Doc spoke suddenly to Renny. A startled expression came over the big engineer's face, then he grinned thinly. He took off the goggles he was wearing.

At the next subway stop, Doc alone appeared when the train came into the station. He got off the rear car. A moment later the two gunmen followed.

A huge shape materialized behind them. It came from the back of the subway train. Enormous fists, used quite often to drive through solid oak doors, reached out. Each fist fastened in a coat collar.

The men clawed frantically for their guns. They seemed unable to reach them. Instead, they sailed backward; were hauled off the rear end of the platform, out of sight. There was a short, decisive flurry. Then Renny returned to the platform, a satisfied smile on his severe features. He was alone. The two gunmen, unconscious, were concealed under the platform.

At the next station, Doc found what he had been looking for. Prints showed their visitor had left the subway at this point. They followed the trail to the street.

As they reached the sidewalk, the wailing siren of a police car could be heard clearly. In the distance was the clamorous gong of an ambulance.

A faint frown creased the forehead of the bronze man.

MONK and Ham got out of their taxi-cab a block from the apartment where Gloria Delpane lived. They had no particular reason for being especially cautious. It was merely habit.

At the far corner of the block was a big black sedan. No one appeared to be in it. But as Monk and Ham came down the sidewalk, a section of the top of the sedan slid back. Light flashed on a mirror.

Monk's long arms were swinging back and forth rapidly. The hairy chemist's small eyes appeared more than ever to be buried in tiny gristles of fat.

"Take it easy," Ham cautioned quietly. "It may be a false alarm. That guy might really have been a photographer."

"And carrying a gun?" Monk demanded reasonably.

"At any rate, we don't want to scare the girl. What we want is the shirt," the dapper lawyer counseled. He stopped to flick a speck of dust from his otherwise immaculate attire.

The apartment was the type where you press a button and the tenant you are calling releases the catch. But in the daytime the outer door often is open. It was unlocked now.

A quick glance at the register showed that Gloria Delpane lived in apartment 4-D. There was an automatic elevator, but it could be heard coming down. Monk and Ham did not wait for it. They went up the stairs rapidly.

The apartment was at the rear. Doc's two aids moved toward it noiselessly. Then they stopped to listen. No sound came from inside.

Ham started to reach for the buzzer, then paused. The door was not fully closed, but was slightly ajar. Monk's eyebrows went up and down; he glanced at Ham. The lawyer nodded.

Monk went across the corridor, crouched down low, just out of line with the door. Ham stood at one side. Then the lawyer reached over and snapped the door wide.

Sp-ff-t!

A bullet from a silenced gun tore through space. It would have hit anyone standing in the doorway.

In the same instant, a burly projectile, bowed low, tore through the doorway in the other direction. The projectile was Monk. He was bent over until his hands trailed the floor. As he reached the doorway, he dived headlong.

Monk's idea had been good. So far as he knew, only the girl was in the apartment. He counted on speed to disarm her without difficulty.

He hadn't counted on the five men who were in the apartment as well as the girl. One stood far back across the room, holding one hand over the girl's mouth. With the other, he held a gun. He had been the one who had fired

Monk caught only a fleeting glimpse of the girl and the man. Then he thought a football team had fallen on him. The other four occupants of the room attacked from all directions.

Blackjacks were swinging for Monk's head. He rolled frantically, queer, rumbling noises coming from his throat.

Ham dived into the room. The cane he carried had changed into a sword. That sword darted in and out rapidly. It caught one burly tough just as he bent over to slam, as hard as he could, at Monk's head.

The tough cursed and moved through the air rapidly. He fell down and apparently went calmly to sleep. The point of Ham's sword contained a swift-acting anaesthetic.

Monk got up. He got up with two men clinging to him. The homely chemist was chuckling almost pleasantly. He caught hold of the two men trying to strangle him and knocked their heads together very hard. They ceased to take an interest in affairs.

The man with the gun was dancing about excitedly, but it was impossible for him to fire without taking the chance of hitting one of his own men. Ham started for him.

That was a mistake. A long, lean, ex-pug appeared in the doorway behind. He had been on the watch, had seen the signal from the sedan and warned the others in the room. He wore brass knuckles on each fist. He set himself and swung.

The knuckles caught Ham just behind the ear. The dapper lawyer never even knew what hit him. Monk whirled—but he whirled just in time to get his jaw in the way of the second pair of brass sleep-makers. He became very quiet and inactive.

Doc also was encountering a crowd, but of a different type. The crowd was in front of an old brownstone house, and consisted mostly of police, detectives and newspapermen. Even the newspapermen were excited. The house was the one where the strange, luminous trail ended.

The bronze man spoke briefly to Renny. The big engineer nodded glumly. The next moment Doc was gone.

A few moments later a figure slipped into the brownstone house from the roof. Doc could have obtained information directly from the police, but that might have brought complications. It was never his policy to advertise his interest in any particular case.

He eased his way down winding stairways and wide halls. But now, not even his aids would have recognized him, though they knew he was an expert at make-up.

Instead of Doc's tall, athletic frame, the man who moved through the house appeared old and bent. His hair was not bronze; it was white. There were deep lines on his face, and his voice was quavering as he encountered a detective.

"B-but what is it, officer?"

The detective snorted. "Nothing for you to worry about, grandpa," he advised condescendingly. "Just a man died, is all."

The old man's eyes blinked. "B-but I never knew that would cause such a stir."

The detective laughed. He stepped aside slightly, so the other could see into the room. A faint, trilling sound came. The detective whirled, stared about wonderingly. When he turned back again the old man was gone.

Doc had seen all that was necessary. The figure in the room the detective was guarding, was that of the man who had called himself Thorne.

A deputy coroner was inspecting the body. The face and body were green. An expression of terrible fear was blazoned on the features. The green death of the Matto Grosso had struck again! The man whom Doc had hoped could give him more information about Johnny, was dead!

Chapter V

GANGSTERS ATTACK

Monk recovered first. The hairy chemist had the impression that he was in a sawmill, with a giant buzzsaw operating close to his head. Finally he decided most of the buzzing was inside, not outside his skull.

He squirmed his squat body around. Ham was stretched out rather inelegantly for once. Monk wished he could have a picture of that; then he turned to more serious affairs.

Rope had been tied tightly about his ankles and his wrists. His wrists were behind him. Ham was similarly bound.

The hairy chemist grunted and went through several contortions, inching his way across the floor until he was close to the lawyer. Then he slammed the heel of one shoe down hard on the floor.

A thin, razor-edged piece of steel shot out of the toe of his shoe. It was held firmly in the leather. It wasn't much of a job for Monk to cut loose the ropes that held Ham. The invention was one of Doc's and had proved its value before.

Ham still showed no signs of returning consciousness. A faint grin split Monk's homely face.

"Sow-e-e-e-e-e-e! Piggy! Piggy! Piggy!" Monk called. His voice was an excellent imitation of a Missouri hogcaller's.

Ham jerked erect. For a moment a startled expression crossed the dapper lawyer's face. Monk bellowed.

"Why, you——" Ham's face became crimson. It wasn't often that he was at a loss for words. He was now. Monk had tricked him.

That hog call was one of Ham's sorest points. It reminded him of World War days when a pig had been stolen and he had received the blame. The nickname "Ham" had resulted from that incident. And Ham always had believed Monk knew more about the stolen pig than he had ever told.

"Sow-e-e-e-e-e-e! Sow-e-e-e-e-e-e!" Monk cooed mockingly.

"I—I ought to leave you tied up, you stone-age throwback," Ham raged. He was still muttering to himself as he freed the hairy chemist.

They were alone in the apartment. That had been apparent from the first. The five men were gone. So was the girl. There was no sign of the missing shirt. A hasty search assured them that almost everything else in the apartment was gone, as well.

Only a discarded frock or two remained in the bedroom closet. There was no sign of other wearing apparel, or of luggage of any kind. The furniture looked surprisingly well-dusted.

Ham drew a small glass from his pocket, inspected some of the furniture, then looked at the doorknob. He nodded soberly. There wasn't a fingerprint to be found. Their attackers had been thorough.

Monk was rummaging in the kitchen. A pint of milk disappeared, as well as the remains of a fried chicken.

"Cooked southern style, too," he chuckled, as Ham caught him. Monk had left none of the chicken for his partner.

Ham snorted sourly, just as a jubilant yell came from Monk. The chemist's hand darted under paper lining on a shelf. He brought out a torn envelope. Then Monk's face fell.

The envelope was empty. Only part of a name remained. That read: "—lcorn."

"What the——" Ham started.

"Scotty Falcorn, the missing aviator," Monk breathed. "The guy who is supposed to have vanished——"

"—in the Matto Grosso section," Ham finished. "And that means the girl is really tied up in this some place. But how?"

Grumbling, they started back to Doc's office.

THEY were not alone in heading for the skyscraper suite of the bronze man. Another also was on the way there. Bowed head covered with an old shawl, bedraggled skirt almost reaching the sidewalk, a bent figure was moving slowly along the crowded street.

Shrewd eyes peered from a lined face, but mostly those

eyes remained down. And despite apparent age and a fragile shape, the old woman made good time.

When she reached the big office building, she hesitated for a moment, moved falteringly toward an elevator. She did not give the number of Doc Savage's floor. She got off a floor below, then moved cautiously up a stairway.

Her shrewd eyes narrowed slightly as she peered down the hallway. Then she drew back, flattening herself out of sight. Two policemen were standing before the bronze man's door.

As she watched, the door swung open and Doc Savage appeared, his face as expressionless as usual. The policemen spoke briefly. What they said could not be heard, but Doc Savage's voice came clearly, although he did not speak loudly.

"No, I am sorry. I have as yet been unable to determine what caused the death of the man here," he said. "I regret that there has been a second victim, as you tell me there has been."

The door closed. The policemen looked baffled, but they turned and went away.

Outside, newspaper extras were black with gigantic headlines:

SECOND EXPLORER IS GREEN DEATH VICTIM

THIRD MEMBER OF BAND SOUGHT BY SCIENTISTS IN EFFORT TO SAFEGUARD LIFE

A peculiar expression appeared on the face of the old woman. The shawl was pulled up tighter about her head. Moving silently, she went down the hall. Then she froze.

A strange, shrill-pitched squeal sounded. It was as though a terrific blast of high-pressure air had been released. Before she could move, an elevator door snapped open and Monk and Ham stepped out. The squeal had been the sound Doc Savage's special, high-speed elevator made as it skyrocketed upward.

A faint gasp came from the old woman. She turned, tried to run.

Monk and Ham saw her at the same moment. A grunt came from Monk. But before he could get his short, squatty frame into action, Ham darted past him.

The old woman moved surprisingly fast. Ham, though, was faster. He overhauled her as if she had been standing still. He reached out and caught her gently.

"Wait a minute——" he began.

Then Ham received a surprise. The small, frail appearing figure erupted into frantic action. Hands clawed, feet lashed out. Ham was forced to let go.

"Can't even hold an old woman," Monk chuckled. Then he also caught hold of the struggling figure. A startled look crossed his homely face. The old woman appeared to have muscles of iron.

Ham's hand swept up. By accident, it caught the shawl, yanked it free. Then Monk stopped trying to be easy. He grabbed the figure with all his strength, lifted it clear off the floor.

Absence of the shawl revealed that the snooper was a man, not a woman. It was a man with an exceptionally large head. Both Monk and Ham recognized their victim at once.

It was Hugo Parks, the third of those who had returned from the Matto Grosso jungle alive.

PARKS was still stuttering furiously as Monk carried him into Doc's office.

Then a surprising thing happened. The instant they were inside the office, Hugo Parks stopped struggling. His eyes, which had been wide with fright, gradually regained a more intelligent look.

"I—I'm sorry," he gasped. "I didn't know who you were, or I wouldn't have fought. For this is where I wanted to come. I wanted to see Doc Savage. I have to! My life is at stake!"

The commotion attracted Doc and Renny. The bronze man stood silently, his gold-flecked eyes emotionless as he surveyed the small figure before him.

"I had expected you," Doc said at last. Renny looked startled. Hugo Parks did not appear to notice.

"Unless you help me, and help me at once, I'll die," the small man wailed. His huge head sagged limply. "I've got to get back—got to get back to the Green Hell district. I've got to!"

"You mean that otherwise the curse will get you, too?" Renny gulped.

Hugo Parks nodded dumbly.

"What about the other white man, Johnny, our friend, whom you saw die?" Doc Savage asked quietly.

An expression of pain came into Parks's eyes. "It—it is true," he said. "We saw him drop, his body turn green. We were being attacked at the time, but we could not have helped him in any case. Later, we found his camp, learned he was one of your men, and found the few objects my companion brought here. There was a lead box, also. It was empty, but I thought it might be valuable. I brought it along. But our rooms here were ransacked. The lead box was taken."

An expression of sadness flitted over the bronze man's features. There was no doubting the sincerity of the other's words.

"And Johnny's body, you recovered that?" he asked.

Hugo Parks shook his head. "W-we tried to, later. It was gone," he said simply. "There are many wild animals there."

A low moan came from Renny. Johnny had been his particular friend. "There isn't any hope at all?" he asked brokenly. Then the big engineer's face hardened. "We can go there," he half shouted. "If his body disappeared, there may be a chance—even though we know there isn't. There must be——"

Doc interrupted quietly. His features and voice again were calm. "Just where is the place to which you must return?" he asked Hugo Parks.

"I won't tell," the large-headed man said unexpectedly.

"What?" Monk and Ham jumped forward. "Our friend died there! You want a favor, and yet——"

"Wait!" the bronze man said. His voice was low, but Monk and Ham stopped instantly. Doc went on: "I gather, then, that what you want is for us to take you back to the Green Hell, but to insure that we do not leave you behind and go at once to hunt for trace of Johnny, you will direct us as we go along. Is that correct?"

Hugo Parks's head wagged energetically. Then fear returned to his features.

"But you will take me? You will take me at once?" he bleated.

Doc turned to his aids. "I believe the dirigible would be best for our purpose," he said quietly.

Monk sighed with relief. He had known what Doc's decision must be. There could be no other course until they had learned for themselves that Johnny was dead. The hairy chemist's fists closed hard. "Maybe we'll run into some action," he breathed.

OTHERS seemed to have the same idea. They were working silently and purposefully. They were in a subbasement garage in the office building where Doc stayed. The garage was used only by the bronze man and his aids.

At least a dozen men were there. Monk and Ham might have recognized several as those they had encountered at Gloria Delpane's apartment. Renny would have recognized two others as those he had tackled in the subway.

One of the men was busy at the big, bulletproof car that Doc drove. He had the hood up, was working with wires near the powerful engine. A second man was directly under the car itself.

Others had scattered about the garage. They found places of concealment and waited nervously. All of them had submachine guns in their hands.

"I—I don't like this," one of them volunteered to his partner. It was one of the pair Renny had manhandled. "This Doc Savage is dynamite."

The other spat softly, shrugged his shoulders. The pin points of his eyes showed he was under the influence of narcotics. He held his Tommy gun with loving hands.

"Orders from the big boss," he said briefly.

The other shivered slightly. "T-this is goin' to be as bad as the St. Valentine's massacre," he muttered. "Only worse. Because these are big shots we'll be bumping."

"And see that you help get them all," the other replied coldly. "The big boy's orders said so, and you know——" He broke off suddenly. A gunman near the elevator shaft had given a signal. The two men about the car closed the hood and darted into hiding. The basement garage became very still.

Air hissed in the elevator shaft, became a roar. The high-speed cage was descending, and it was coming down fast. Only Chemistry and Habeas Corpus had been left behind. Monk and Ham were to return for them later.

Renny held the frail figure of Hugo Parks, kept the huge-headed man from leaving the floor as the elevator dropped out from under him. Monk and Ham grinned slightly.

Doc pressed a control button. The elevator stopped so suddenly that all except the bronze man involuntarily bent at the knees. The door opened.

Concealed figures grew tense. Fingers were ready on the triggers of Tommy guns.

Doc stepped out. The others followed. The bronze man's eyes swept the garage. His pace did not falter, but he shifted direction slightly.

"We need more light," he said calmly, and reached for a button on the wall.

Then things happened!

SOMEONE shouted an order. The basement was filled with the wicked roar of Tommy guns. A rain of death beat toward the figures of Doc and his aids.

But the bronze man had moved too fast.

With one quick sweep he had hit the button on the wall. In the next instant he had hurled his powerful frame sideways. He struck with the speed and power of an expert football blocker. But his body was entirely off the floor and was going far swifter than even a clever blocker moves.

He knocked Hugo Parks, Monk, Ham and Renny from their feet. They went to the floor just as hot lead swept over them.

Then the Tommy guns stopped. A fog appeared to have filled the basement in a fraction of a second. The fog was a quick-acting anesthetic gas released when Doc had hit the button on the wall. The bronze man alone had noticed small, significant factors when they entered the garage. A barrel had been moved. A light that should have been on was off.

Doc flashed to his feet. He was holding his breath. So were Monk, Ham and Renny. They had understood what

Doc was doing when he had reached for the wall button. They were unaffected by the gas.

The bronze man motioned orders. Renny picked up the unconscious figure of Hugo Parks. They raced for the big car in the center of the garage. Doc dived behind the wheel.

Air was necessary, and that very shortly. For once, the bronze man had been caught without the oxygen tablets he usually carried. And while he could hold his breath for minutes, his aids could not. They would soon be overcome.

Swiftly, Doc stepped on the car starter. The electrical contact did its work. A powerful bomb exploded beneath the machine.

Chapter VI

A STOWAWAY

BEFORE the crash of the explosion had died out, doors, controlled by electric eyes, opened. The big car, driven by Doc Savage, sped up a ramp to the fresh air of the street.

Monk, Ham and Renny had been groggy even before the blast. The terrific burst of sound had left them dazed. It was several seconds before they recovered enough to marvel at their escape.

Before they could ask questions, Doc had stopped the car. Swiftly, he was out into the street, had dived back into the subcellar garage. The place looked as if it had been struck by a hurricane of more than ordinary strength. Oil cans, heavy machinery, a small car—all had been hurled to the side walls.

The luckless gangsters had been trapped beneath the heavy equipment. Only two of them were still alive, and they were severely hurt.

Doc's face did not change expression. He turned on fans that would clear the air within a few minutes. Then he went to a telephone, gave a number. When the connection had been made, he gave brief instructions. Without a backward glance he turned and left the place.

An ambulance would soon arrive. It would be a private ambulance. The two surviving thugs would take a trip in that. They would go to an upstate sanitarium that few knew Doc owned. There, they would undergo skilled operations. When they recovered, they would be released without memory of their previous criminal occupations, ready to take their places as respectable citizens.

Before the ambulance left, a call would be made to the police. The cops would face another mystery.

Hugo Parks was sitting up when Doc got back to the car. The large-headed man's complexion was pasty. He had appeared frightened before. Now he was plainly terrified. His eyes darted nervously from side to side; his tongue wet dry lips.

"Why was an attempt made to kill us?" Doc asked quietly.

The other swallowed hard and shook his head. "I—I don't know," he stammered. There was no doubting his desperate earnestness.

"Why should anyone here be mixed up in Matto Grosso? What would their connection be with the green death?" Ham demanded. The dapper lawyer snapped his question in his best cross-examination manner.

Again Hugo Parks shook his head. "There couldn't be any connection," he said fiercely, almost too emphatically. Ham got the sudden notion the other was trying to convince himself that this was a fact.

The attack was just one more of a whole series of puzzling events that seemed to have no connecting link, but which must be tied up with the green death some way, Ham decided. For a moment, his expression was as set and stern as that of Renny's.

Doc slid behind the wheel, spun the car around and headed for the North River.

Monk's curiosity could wait no longer. "That was a bomb that went off under this car, wasn't it?" he asked accusingly.

Doc nodded. A faint glint that might have been amusement appeared in his gold-flecked eyes.

"Then what I want to know," Monk piped demandingly, "is why we didn't all get blown up, daggonit?"

"Molecular resistance," Doc said briefly.

The hairy chemist's eyes widened. "Molecular re—— But I still don't see!"

"The type of explosive bomb used under autos always exerts its force upward," Doc explained. He slowed down as the car neared a big warehouse bearing the name "HIDALGO TRADING COMPANY."

Doc continued: "The underneath side of this car is lined with containers of a compressed gas that, when once released, exerts a tremendous downward pressure. The bomb exploded. It freed the compressed gas, which blocked the upward charge of the explosive, forcing it to seek escape in other directions. In this case, that direction was toward each side."

The expression on Monk's face was a tribute in itself. The homely chemist could imagine what had happened inside the garage.

Doc stopped the car before the warehouse. "We'll get the dirigible ready," he said.

The others alighted, glanced around swiftly. They saw nothing. There was a taxicab a block away, but it appeared deserted. They did not see the girl huddled down in the rear seat.

The girl left the cab as soon as Doc and the others disappeared into the warehouse. She carried a small bundle under one arm and moved along the waterfront street as inconspicuously as possible.

It was just growing dusk. Trucks were rolling up in front of the warehouse, in response to orders from Doc; supplies were being unloaded rapidly and carried inside. For a time, the girl clung to the security of a sheltered doorway across the street. A truck drove away. For a moment there was no one in sight.

Swiftly she darted across the street and into the warehouse.

A hundred yards away, a man appeared. He just missed seeing the girl. He also slid down the street, taking care not to be seen. He whistled softly. A second figure joined him from the opposite direction.

Waiting their chance, they, too, slipped into the big warehouse.

Ordinarily, such easy entrance would have been impossible. But in the speed of loading, Doc had disconnected his regular alarm systems.

ONCE inside, the girl seemed bewildered. The place had appeared dilapidated from the street. It did not appear to contain anything of value. That was a mistake.

There was a big yacht in a concrete dry dock. Near by was a submarine, close to a ramp was a speedy amphibian, with a fast-racing plane now attached to its back. A small gyroplane rested close by. And held some twenty feet off the ground was a cigar-shaped dirigible.

Rope ladders ran from the dirigible, except at one point. There, a landing platform had been built, rising high from the floor. Supplies were being carried up to this platform. A majority of the lights were there, also. Men could be seen working busily.

The girl's breath came in sharply. She darted to the far side of the big warehouse, clinging to the shadows. The dark dress she wore made her almost invisible.

Doc and his men were busy. Only Hugo Parks was taking no part in the activity. He was crouched back in the lounge room of the dirigible, making himself as small as possible. Perspiration glistened on his features. He glanced around with constant nervousness.

The last load of provisions came aboard. There was a moment of confusion as a workman dropped a loaded case. The girl chose that moment to dart up a rope ladder at the far side of the dirigible. She slipped inside, found a hiding place in a small closet. Only one pair of eyes noticed her arrival.

No one at all saw the two men, now also opposite the dirigible. They worked swiftly, as if they knew what they were doing. One ran what appeared to be a long snake along the warehouse floor, then attached it to the dirigible. His companion was busy near the far wall.

"These guys may be pretty good, but not even the big bronze devil can dodge what is going to happen," the one by the wall chuckled.

"WE'RE all set to go," Renny said primly.

A sigh of relief came from Hugo Parks. For a moment the large-headed man looked more human. "The quicker the better," he breathed.

Monk and Ham started to move toward the landing platform. "Just one thing we forgot," the chemist piped. "I'll be back in a few minutes."

"You mean two things we forgot," Ham put in belligerently. "We'll *both* be back in a few——"

The man at the far wall of the warehouse grinned sourly. Monk's and Ham's voices came clearly.

"You mean you're not goin' anywhere at all," he muttered. He slammed a switch.

There was a terrific flash. Lightning played about the dirigible; streaks of flame raced about the framework, made the big, metal bag appear outlined in dancing fire.

A shriek came from Hugo Parks. The large-headed man understood what that meant. A high-voltage line had been hooked to the framework of the big airship. Parks thought of the Hindenburg disaster. He remembered other airships that had been stricken in the sky, to fall flaming, burning all on board.

He leaped up, started to race toward an exit so he could leap from the dirigible.

Monk had just reached out one hand to grab a rail to steady himself when the man-made lightning bolt struck. Had his hand been on metal, there would have been no chance for him. Even so, his fist was so close that a spark jumped. The hairy chemist felt as if a gigantic mule had kicked him. He went sailing backward, end over end.

His hurtling figure smashed into the smaller frame of Hugo Parks. The little man went down very suddenly. The air had the dry, ozone smell that always accompanies lightning or a severe electrical disturbance.

Doc Savage was a blur of motion. The bronze man donned a rubber suit so rapidly his movements could hardly be seen. The next instant he had dropped from the gondola of the dirigible.

The twenty-foot fall did not appear to disturb him in the least. He landed with powerful legs bent slightly at the knees, and his enormous muscles absorbed the shock with ease.

Seconds later, the electrical fireworks vanished. Doc found where the high-powered line had been attached to the framework. One tremendous yank pulled the wire free.

Monk, Ham and Renny went into action without hesitation. An attempt had been made to kill them. That meant the attackers must still be in the warehouse.

Each seized a queer-appearing weapon. A huge drum surmounted a pistol. Those who had fought Doc in the past knew what those weapons were. They fired with a bull-fiddle roar, sending out a stream of bullets. The bullets did not kill, but merely brought unconsciousness.

From somewhere close at hand, an automatic spat flame. Hot lead whizzed close to Monk.

The homely chemist's finger tightened on the trigger of his weapon. The roar filled the warehouse with thunderous echoes.

The two would-be killers were close together. They had not thought to run until the electrical display stopped. They had wanted to be sure that Doc and his aids were killed.

Now they made a move toward the distant door. A thunderbolt seemed to hit them from behind. Doc, difficult to see in the rubber suit he wore, had circled behind them. Each powerful hand caught the neck of one of the two gangsters.

Ordinarily that grip would have been sufficient. Doc could bring unconsciousness by hitting certain nerves in the neck of a foe. But the big rubber gloves he still wore were too bulky.

The men yanked free and started to run. Doc was on them at once. This time, a fist shot out. A man screamed and dodged catching hold of his companion as he went to the floor.

There was a vivid flash—then silence. The man had fallen on the exposed end of the high-tension wire. He and his companion had been electrocuted instantly.

THE dirigible should have been destroyed; only precautions taken by Doc had saved it. It was filled with noncombustible helium, for one thing; and for another, it always had an electrical ground when moored in the warehouse. Electricity had raced through the metal framework and then had been carried off, leaving the big airship undamaged.

Hugo Parks was still cowering in fear. He understood now that if Monk had not knocked him down, he would have been killed when he touched the metal railing of the ship.

Doc examined the bodies of the two men who had been killed. There was nothing he could do for them. Then he gave brief instructions to Ham. The dapper lawyer led Hugo Parks from the dirigible, forced him to look at the two bodies.

"Know either of these two?" Ham demanded.

The large-headed man appeared to become even more

pale. He wet his lips feverishly, while his eyes rolled as if seeking more attackers.

"N-no," he stammered.

Ham growled, started to ask another question. Doc shook his head slightly. The lawyer's mouth closed. Ham was sure Hugo Parks had lied. He knew Doc also thought that. But if Doc wanted to make the other think he was believed, that was all right with him.

The whole thing was screwy; it was getting crazier by the minute. But there was serious business to attend to. Explanations could wait.

Johnny undoubtedly was dead. But there could be no peace of mind for Doc and his aids until they knew for sure, and until they had done all that could be done.

Hugo Parks remained on the dirigible. There was no questioning his fear—he was a man shaken with panic. Doc and Renny also stayed about. Monk and Ham made a quick trip to Doc's office.

When they returned, they were in better humor. They had Habeas Corpus and Chemistry with them, as well as certain supplies Doc had requested. Habeas was squealing with delight. He knew a trip was about to start, and for a pig, Habeas almost seemed to think. Chemistry deserted Ham to cling adoringly to Monk's arm. The ape had much affection for the homely chemist.

Just at midnight the big doors of the warehouse swung open, controlled automatically. Machinery "walked" the dirigible out. A few moments later it had cast off and soon was rising slowly over the Hudson.

In the darkened closet, a very good-looking girl made herself as comfortable as possible. There was a look of grim determination on her features.

The mysteries of Matto Grosso and the green death lay ahead, but no hint of the seriousness of the trip showed on the features of Doc and his aids. All were worried about Johnny, but long ago they had realized that sooner or later they would go on one adventure too many; that some of their loyal group would fall victims to death.

It was too bad it had to be serious-minded Johnny. It was worse that he had fallen while on a comparatively peaceful trip of exploration.

But none believed that this was all there was to it. There had to be something else. The attacks made on them in New York, the appearance of the horrible green death there, all showed that. Danger loomed ahead, but that would come when they reached the Green Hell region.

There was no need for advice from Hugo Parks on the first part of the trip. The dirigible headed south, with Renny at the controls. The others went to sleep.

That is, all but one did. Some time during the night, a cabin door opened; a dim figure made a cautious trip through the dirigible, then returned.

Habeas Corpus was sniffing around. In particular he stayed near the door of a seldom-used closet. But neither Monk nor Ham were awake to notice that.

At daybreak, Doc relieved Renny, who promptly fell into deep slumber. The big engineer rested easily. There was no danger for the present, of that he was sure.

It was at that moment the attack came. It struck without warning. Two speedy pursuit ships, machine guns blazing, dived on the dirigible from above.

Chapter VII

A DESERTION

THE gunners in the pursuit ships expected an easy victory. They were shooting incendiary bullets. They knew those bullets could not set fire to helium, but they would start flames if they touched wood or hit the fuel tanks of the dirigible. And the dirigible appeared slow compared with the high speed of the diving planes.

Then the gunners received their first surprise. The big bag below them rolled slightly back and forth. The tracer bullets did not penetrate, but merely glanced off the sides.

It took some seconds for them to realize that the airship did not have the ordinary type of bag, but that the helium was contained in a thin, extremely tough but light type of metal. The bullets were striking at an angle and richocheting.

As soon as that was apparent, the planes pulled up, rolled, and dived straight down. Bullets fired straight at the metal bag of the dirigible would have no chance to glance.

Then the pilots received their second surprise. The dirigible apparently vanished. A moment before it had been speeding along, directly below them. Now there was nothing in the sky to see.

One of the pilots swore. His hard face was reckless. There was a shade of worry there, also. His orders had been explicit —the dirigible must be destroyed! Doc Savage must be halted!

The pilot threw his pursuit ship into a screaming dive. With the prop roaring like a thousand banshees, he sped toward the rolling sea beneath.

A shout came suddenly from his lips. He yanked the stick of the plane so hard that he thought for a moment he had pulled off the wings. He barely cleared the dirigible.

The pilot had shouted when he had seen another plane speeding up toward him at as fast a rate as he was diving.

The pilot's reflexes were good. He'd acted just in time. And he knew, now, why he had lost sight of the big airship.

Doc had released a thin gas. The gas had acted as a mirror, hiding the dirigible beneath it. The angle of the sun's rays had combined to give the impression that there was nothing in sight.

The pilot was angry. The "ship" he had seen zooming toward him had been a reflection of his own diving plane. He yanked back on the stick, pulled his ship up until it was standing on its tail. Lead roared toward the belly of the airship.

THERE was much activity aboard the dirigible. Monk, Ham and Renny had rolled out the instant they had heard the first shots fired. Chemistry and Habeas also were racing back and forth excitedly.

Only Doc, at the controls, appeared calm.

All aboard knew the dirigible stood no chance of outrunning the attackers that were harrying it. The dirigible was built with a long cruising range, and did have more than ordinary speed—but far from enough to compete with pursuit ships.

But Doc's aids were unworried. The situation looked bad; but they knew the bronze man.

Hugo Parks *was* worried. His eyes shone with fear. He made no effort to help the others beat off the attack. Instead, his actions were strange.

The small man slipped along a corridor, glancing about constantly to make sure he was not observed.

Then he ducked into the radio room. Once inside, he seemed to know just what to do. His actions were those of a professional radio operator.

For a moment he stood motionless before the set, studying it with shrewd eyes. Then he nodded, and a satisfied smile widened his lips. He had expected the set to be one of the most modern in the world. It was.

Swiftly he changed several adjustments. The wave length he used was far below the usual bands, down so low, in fact, that ordinarily he would have needed an especially-built set to reach it. He didn't this time. Doc's set could be adjusted to touch almost any known wave length—and some that weren't so well-known.

Tubes hummed softly. Hugo Parks looked around anxiously, then smiled again. There was no danger of being interrupted. The others were too busy to notice that the radio was being used.

Then he slipped on a set of headphones, pulled a microphone toward him. He plugged the mike in, and a thin film of perspiration covered his face.

"Calling S-N," he croaked. "Calling S-N." Over and over he repeated the call.

Outside, the tide of battle was raging swiftly. Monk, Ham and Renny had put machine guns into action. Lead poured back at the attackers, forcing them to use more care.

The large-headed man paid no heed. Sweat now was literally running from his face. His voice was hoarse. "Calling S-N," he repeated.

He jerked in his chair. His jaw went slack. Then a long sigh came from him. His shoulders relaxed.

An answer had come over the headphones.

Hugo Parks talked swiftly and at length. His voice was hurt, almost plaintive.

The earphones crackled. Hugo Parks's eyes became large. He seemed to wilt.

"Yes, S-N," he breathed. "Yes, sir; I understand. It—it's awful. B-but I'll do my part. I'll do as you say."

Slowly he removed the headphones from his ears. Still acting as though he were punch-drunk, he restored the radio set to its original wave length.

He staggered from the room. His movements were awkward, his eyes glazed, as though he had received a sentence of death.

At the controls of the dirigible, Doc's low, trilling sound came. The bronze man's gold-flecked eyes were narrowed. There was a small loud-speaker almost at his ear. He had overheard Hugo Parks's conversation.

Then his attention came back to the fight.

MACHINE guns, expertly wielded by Doc's aids, had forced the attacking planes to use caution. But the dirigible had "blind" spots. The three could not always be where they could cover the airship from all angles.

And the pilots evidently had come to the conclusion that bullets alone, even incendiary ones, would not be sufficient to down the dirigible.

They were dropping bombs. Climbing high above the airship, almost invisible in the sky, but keeping directly on the course of their target, they dropped explosive missiles of death. Their target was a comparatively simple one.

Skillful manipulation of controls by Doc caused the first two bombs to drop by harmlessly and explode in the sea beneath. But not even the bronze man's great skill could forestall eventual defeat.

The bombs were small but powerful. They were hard to see with the naked eye, and traveled so fast it was difficult to get the big airship out of the way.

Doc called to Renny. The big engineer leaped to the controls.

The bronze man dived toward the stern of the ship. Soon he had pulled a queer-shaped object into view. In appearance, it was something like an ancient blunderbuss, except that the muzzle flared even wider, being almost two feet across. A large tank was attached to it.

Four small bombs started down at once. It was impossible for the dirigible to dodge them all.

Renny's thin, disapproving lips were more tightly compressed than usual. He nodded as Doc gave a signal.

The next instant the dirigible swung on its side as Renny's powerful muscles manipulated levers, changing the ballast.

The blunderbuss-appearing weapon pointed straight up. Doc pressed a lever. A sheet of flame swept skyward. It was a tremendous blanket of fire, starting a good two hundred feet above the dirigible and extending for yards on all sides.

There were four powerful explosions as the bombs plunged into the flame and were discharged. Bits of steel rained down harmlessly.

Doc turned a petcock. The flame broadened until it seemed to cover the sky, forming a protective curtain high above the dirigible.

It was then the attacking pilots made the first and last

real error. They thought at least one bomb must have struck the dirigible; that it had exploded. They dived down to make sure.

They had expected the flame to vanish. The sudden increase in the fire caught them by surprise. Before they could whip their planes up, they ran into the blanket of crimson destruction. A moment more and their ships were plunging on downward, flaming coffins.

One of the pilots tried to jump with his parachute. The parachute caught fire before he could leave his ship. He stood no chance.

Doc's gold-flecked eyes were regretful. He did not like to take human life. He had not intended to do so. Only the savage vengefulness of the pilots was to blame. They had been too anxious to see the destruction they thought they had caused.

They could have turned and fled; but they had not. So they paid with their lives for the error.

As the hours slipped by, only Hugo Parks appeared restless. The others were more seasoned travelers.

Monk and Ham amused themselves with Chemistry and Habeas Corpus. Renny was usually at the controls of the dirigible. Doc spent most of his time in the well-equipped laboratory he had aboard the airship.

His aids did not bother him with questions. They knew that when the bronze man got ready to explain, he would— and not before. They were sure that whatever he was working on must have some connection with the mysterious green death.

They would really have been mystified had they been watching. Doc was studying and testing fingernail parings. They were thin, ordinary-appearing, except for one thing: they were green. They had come from the man who had been mummified at Doc's office.

The recent escape from the attacking planes brought little comment from Doc's aids. They understood the weapon he had used. It had merely been a highly-developed flame-thrower, using a thin type of inflammable gas that would float in the air and spread rapidly, yet still produce terrific heat.

Gradually the coast line changed beneath them. Then they were over land. Soon afterwards, Hugo Parks began spending more of his time near Renny and the maps before the big engineer.

They were rapidly approaching Brazil.

Habeas Corpus was feeling indolent. Warm weather always affected him that way. Chemistry was more chipper than ever. The climate was to his liking. And the ape had invented a new game.

He would wait until Habeas was sleeping soundly, then slip up silently, catch the pig by one long ear, and pound his head on the deck.

Squealing angrily, Habeas would leap up, lower his head and charge. Chemistry would wait until the pig almost was upon him, then leap for ropes that led upward from the gondola. Chattering mockingly, he would hang there until Habeas gave up and went back to sleep.

Ham roared with laughter. Monk glowered. Habeas was his particular pet. It irked him to see the pig getting the worst of a deal.

"But he does have a mentality just like yours," he assured Ham.

The dapper lawyer smiled insultingly. "At least Chemistry has a sense of humor, which is more than can be said for one who looks like him," Ham purred.

The bickering continued. Neither had an inkling as to what was to result from Chemistry's game.

Hugo Parks went by them. They paid no heed, for they were accustomed to seeing the large-headed man wander about the ship. Habeas suddenly roused himself, grunted, and took out in pursuit.

"Looks like you've lost the affections of your pet," Ham jibed. Monk merely scowled.

Hugo Parks paid no attention to the pig. He slipped down the corridor until he reached the door of a small closet. After looking around carefully, he opened the door, put his head inside.

"Tonight," he said briefly. "We can't wait any longer."

He handed the girl a small packet. "You know what to do." He closed the door and went away. Habeas stood there for a long time.

AT dusk, Monk went to the small galley. Ham said it was because Monk was a chemist and knew how to prepare elaborate mixtures in a laboratory, but at any rate he could turn out an excellent meal.

Coffee was his particular delight. He permitted no one to assist him in preparing that, though he did use Hugo Parks as a waiter.

Soon after Monk started the meal, Doc went to the radio room. Hugo Parks noticed that, looked scared suddenly, and crept down the hall after him.

He could hear Doc's voice, but could not make out the words. His eyes were anxious, his face drawn. He glanced at his watch, then turned his gaze nervously toward the direction of the closet door.

A moment later Hugo Parks summoned Monk. "There's a strange-appearing light. It may mean another attack," he said. He hid his nervousness. He appeared excited.

Monk grumbled, but left the galley. With Parks, Monk went to where he could see the sky. The large-headed man kept up a constant chatter. Monk interrupted disgustedly. There was nothing to be seen. Finally they decided it had been a false alarm. Soon afterwards, dinner was served.

Monk himself served the coffee. He wouldn't even let anyone else do that. But he did agree that Parks could take a cup to Renny at the controls. The evening was cool.

Doc's eyes were emotionless, his face without expression.

Ham grimaced as he took the first swallow of his coffee. "Trying a stone-age chemical on us instead of coffee?" he inquired sardonically.

Color flared in Monk's face. Criticism of his coffee was one thing he couldn't stand. He grabbed his cup, drained it almost at a swallow. "It's excellent——" he started. Then he, too, made a face. "What the——" he exclaimed.

"I think it is fine, Monk," said Doc. He finished his cup.

A sleepy expression already was crossing Ham's face. His eyes closed. Monk made a desperate effort to get to his feet, his complexion pasty.

"Drugged!" he gasped. He tried to turn toward Hugo Parks. The large-headed man scurried away.

Doc's eyelids blinked. The bronze man got to his feet,

took two steps. Slowly, his knees folded under him. He went to the floor.

There was a big thump as Renny folded up, hands sliding weakly from the controls.

A nasty grin crossed Hugo Parks's face. He became very busy. He rushed into Doc's laboratory, grabbed several cans. The cans were marked, "GASOLINE—HIGH TEST."

He poured the liquid throughout the main lounge and over the clothing of Doc and his aids. Habeas and Chemistry looked on wonderingly, sniffing at the unaccustomed smell of the gas.

Then Parks fixed a candle so it would burn down and ignite the gasoline within a few minutes. He raced to the closet, threw the door open.

"Come on! It worked!" he exclaimed exultantly.

Gloria Delpane emerged. She appeared rather pale. It had been suffocatingly hot in the closet. She started to speak, but Parks gave her no chance. He grabbed her by the hand, pulled her with him.

A trapdoor opened at the bottom of the gondola. A swift plane was anchored there, with cleverly arranged windbreaks protecting it from the weather and streamlining it so that it did not act as a drag on the dirigible.

Parks pulled the girl into a cockpit. Then he sat at the stick, worked a self-starter. The motor roared. Waiting only long enough to warm up the engine, Parks reached for a lever overhead, gave it a hard jerk. The plane came free, dived for a moment, then straightened out as the large-headed man opened the throttle and the propeller bit into the air.

The swift plane went away from the dirigible rapidly. There was a sudden burst of flame behind them. The airship appeared like a ball of fire. Parks grinned as that ball of flame dived toward the rough land beneath.

"Old-fashioned methods are really better than scientific stuff," he told himself. "Knockout drops in coffee and plain gasoline did the work. Doc Savage is gone." His smile widened. It made his face appear satanic. "And now the green death can really do its stuff," he said jubilantly.

Chapter VIII

FALSE TRAIL

HUGO PARKS took a compass bearing and changed the course of the plane. The direction he took would carry him to a point far distant from that toward which the dirigible had been headed.

The large-headed man set an automatic pilot, then began investigating the instrument board. He grunted with satisfaction as he found a radio. He had expected there would be one. Once again, he changed the wave length. He was answered almost at once.

"It worked!" he gloated. "Doc Savage is past tense. I'll be with you soon after dawn."

Then he shut off the radio. It was not always wise to carry on extended two-way conversations. There was little likelihood that anyone was listening in; but just on the chance that someone was, it wouldn't do to stay on the air long enough for them to take radio bearings and find out where the talk was coming from.

Miles away, another man also shut off his radio transmitter, and with equal satisfaction. He was a tall, well-built man, with shiny black hair plastered tight to his head. The clothes he wore would have won an admiring glance even from the sartorially-perfect Ham.

There was jungle on all sides. The air was steamy and hot, but the sleek man did not appear to notice. A large electric fan provided him some degree of coolness. Electric fans are rather rare in jungles, even in the most luxuriously outfitted exploring parties.

But then, "Sleek" Norton did not appear much like the usual explorer. He sipped a highball from an iced glass, and permitted his eyes to close. A gratified smile split his face. Doc Savage was dead. That was fine. And with the green death——

His smile widened. Of course, he had nothing to fear in any case, he assured himself, but he was just as well satisfied that the bronze man was out of the way.

Had either Sleek Norton or Hugo Parks been equipped with the right type of a televisor, they would have been surprised. For a dead man, Doc Savage was strangely active.

THE bronze man had never been unconscious. He had only pretended to drink the drugged coffee. He was on his feet as soon as Hugo Parks left the dirigible.

The huge ball of flame the large-headed man had seen had been merely a cloud of burning gas, ejected from the flamethrower. With all lights extinguished on the dirigible, Hugo Parks had been fooled completely.

Doc Savage paid no attention to the burning candle on the floor. He acted swiftly to revive his aids. They had been given, he knew, the common type of knockout drops. Ordinary treatment in such cases is to use a stomach pump.

The bronze man went to his laboratory, mixed a small vial of colorless liquid. The liquid had a powerful, penetrating odor. He held it under Renny's nose.

The big engineer's body jerked as though he had been given a jolt of electricity. His eyes opened and he leaped up, huge fists opening and closing.

"Where are they? Where are they?" he shouted. "Who hit me over the head with a blackjack?"

Doc did not reply. He went to where Monk and Ham lay sprawled. The colorless liquid had the same effect on them.

The ordinary knockout drops drug the brain, getting into the bloodstream through the stomach. Doc used a powerful counterirritant, one that poured oxygen into the system and provided such a heavy jolt to blood vessels feeding the brain that it cleared the poison out almost immediately.

"You poisoner!" Ham shouted. "Tried to kill us with that coffee, didn't you?"

"It wasn't the coffee, you shyster," Monk bleated. "You must have been making a speech. Nothing else could put me to sleep so quick."

Ham sputtered. Then he noticed the burning candle and caught the odor of gasoline. The candle flame had almost reached the liquid beneath it.

The lawyer gave a startled squawk and dived toward the candle, putting it out with his fingers.

"That was unnecessary," Doc said quietly.

"But the gas——" Ham began. He stopped, and his face became a redder hue. He didn't care to intimate, even by indirection, that Doc might have overlooked a possible peril.

"It is not gasoline," the bronze man explained quietly. "Had Parks not been in such a rush, he might have discovered it was only water with a perfectly harmless deodorant in it that made it smell like gasoline."

"Parks! Then he did do this?" Monk rasped. "Daggonit, I been suspicious of that guy. He leaped to his feet, swung his long arms, his face contorting in a quiet hideous scowl. "Where is he? Let me at him."

"He took the plane and left—and the girl with him," Doc said quietly.

"The girl?" Monk's face became scarlet. It was his duty to search the ship for stowaways. He had been lax, for he had not done so.

He dived from the room. Habeas Corpus was dancing about in the corridor. When the pig saw Monk, he grunted, trotted swiftly away. Monk hesitated, then followed.

Habeas stopped before the open door of the closet. "Even Habeas had sense enough to know there was someone hiding on board," Ham put in, forgetting that he also had not known it.

Monk did not reply. He had turned on a light inside the closet. A moment later he gave a jubilant yell, raced back into view.

In his hand he held the shirt that had been stolen from the body in Doc's office.

Doc's explanation was brief and concise. He told of overhearing the radio conversation.

"But what is it all about?" Ham asked.

The bronze man shook his head. "That was not disclosed in the conversation," he replied. "Parks was told only to lead us on a false trail and to escape if possible."

"And we let him get away," Renny moaned.

"Certainly, otherwise we would have been taken to an entirely different destination," the bronze man said.

"But the girl? And how are we to know where to go?" Monk put in.

"I did not know of the girl until it was too late to interfere without upsetting our plans," Doc explained. "It was necessary to let Parks think he was really escaping, so he would go to the right place."

"Then we can follow him?" Ham asked.

Doc did not reply in words. He led the way to the control cabin. Beside the wheel was a box resembling a compass. But the needle was not pointing north. It was turned toward the southwest.

"Radio impulses are being constantly discharged by the plane," Doc said. "This needle picks up the waves, points in the direction being followed by the plane."

A wide smile split Renny's stern features. "Holy cow!" he exclaimed. "Then all we have to do is follow the course that is laid out for us."

"And Parks won't ever know we're following," Monk said happily. "Just wait until I get my hands on the big-headed mug. I'll teach him to spoil good coffee!"

Doc Savage said nothing. He took the shirt that had been found in the closet and returned to his laboratory.

There was a faint odor about the shirt, but if it had contained a poison or any other death agent, that poison had been removed. Over the heart a thin piece of cloth had been split. It would have been possible to conceal something there. If there had been anything, however, it was gone.

The bronze man did not appear concerned. He used an instrument similar to that he had brought into play at his New York office. The instrument sucked in air, including that which bore the faint odor that hung about the shirt.

When he had a tube full of this air, Doc set about to analyze it. Sometime later, he completed his work. A paper was filled with chemical symbols. Then he worked out a formula. From the formula, he prepared a vial of reddish-colored liquid.

It was about then that the loudspeaker in the radio room came to life.

"New York calling Doc Savage! New York calling Doc Savage!" the loudspeaker blared.

HUGO PARKS was not listening to the radio on the plane. It is doubtful he would have heard the call even if he had been wearing headphones. The receiver on the plane was good, but its range was far from that of the set on the dirigible.

The large-headed man was watching the country beneath. A bright moon aided him. When he picked up a stream, he seemed relieved, swung the plane to follow the course of the water. It was the River of Death.

The country beneath was wild enough. There were big trees and dense underbrush. Occasionally there would be open spaces, but these were few and far between. Sometimes a startled animal would gaze up at the winged thing which roared above. Some of the animals appeared man-killers.

Parks held steadily to his course throughout the night. The girl slept. When she awakened, she donned the speaking equipment that enabled her to talk to the pilot.

Her eyes were haggard and worried, her face wan. She had endured much in the last few days.

"Are we almost there?" she asked.

"Only another hour," Parks promised. "Then you will find what you wish to find."

For a moment Gloria Delpane's eyes lighted; she appeared beautiful despite the strain. "B-but was it really necessary to kill Doc Savage and his men?" she asked.

"They were our enemies. It had to be done," Parks assured her.

"But I have heard they were very resourceful. Might it not be that they are still alive?" The girl seemed to be voicing what she hoped, rather than what she believed.

"Not a chance," Hugo Parks said.

But a frown crossed his face. Doc Savage was known to be resourceful. Parks thought of it as tricky. And now that he remembered all that had occurred, it seemed his escape and the apparent destruction of the dirigible had been almost too easy.

His brain worked swiftly. He tried to put himself in Doc Savage's place. If the bronze man had had a suspicion all was not as it should be, then he would have permitted him to escape, Parks decided. In that case, then Doc Savage must have a sure way of trailing the plane.

Hugo Parks swore harshly. That must be it. And in the air he had no chance of going over the plane, of trying to find any concealed device that might be giving a clue to their whereabouts.

Then an evil grin lighted the large-headed man's features. Doc Savage was smart, all right, but evidently the bronze man had underestimated Brains. Hugo Parks chuckled.

Others were having doubts of Doc's demise at about the same time. In his comfortable quarters, protected by mosquito netting from flying insects, Sleek Norton was awakened by a radio operator.

"I let you sleep, boss, as long as I could," the man apologized. "But you know Parks said Doc Savage and his dirigible had been destroyed."

"Yes?" Sleek Norton's voice was a snarl. Being awakened at an early hour did not agree with his disposition.

The radio operator gulped. "I—I don't think he is, boss!" he stammered. "I heard New York calling for the bronze devil during the night. At first I didn't think there was any answer, but after a while I got it. Somebody was sending in code, and sending so fast that only a mechanical receiver could get it. I could only make out a word or two."

Sleek Norton's face contorted angrily. "Out with it! What did you think you heard?"

"Well, I got two of the words—'green death,'" the other sputtered. "And the signature sounded to me like 'Clark Savage, Jr.'"

Sleek Norton swore long and fiercely. Then gradually his temper faded and he grinned. "Okay, mug," he said. "It's not your fault. And in any case, that bronze upstart doesn't know where we are—and won't if Brains does his stuff."

HUGO PARKS was doing just that. At his instructions, Gloria Delpane donned a parachute. Her face was white, but her lips were set in a hard, determined line.

The large-headed man also put on a chute. Five miles from a cleared area, he set the automatic pilot on the ship.

As the plane went over the clearing, he told the girl to jump. She did. A moment later Parks followed.

The plane, motors roaring with undiminished beat, continued on through the sky. It was at a high altitude. It had gasoline enough to carry it for at least another thousand miles before the motors died and it crashed.

"Let Doc Savage follow that if he wants," Hugo Parks chuckled. "He'll never find us here!"

Chapter IX

A MESSAGE FROM THE DEAD

THE dirigible also was over the jungle, but it was many miles away. Its speed was far less than that of the plane Parks had stolen.

But no ordinary observer would have even realized the dirigible was in the sky.

Instead, all that could be seen was a cloud. The cloud was moving along at a fast clip, high in the air. In fact, it moved astoundingly fast for a cloud. However, that was not so unusual. Quite often clouds fall into currents of rapidly-moving air, high up, when near the surface leaves in trees are barely stirring.

The cloud was one of Doc's devising. It contained a little moisture, just enough to give it weight, but it also was electrified. The electricity it contained kept it clinging close to the metal shell of the airship.

One or another of Doc's aids was always at the controls. The big ship was kept on a direct course, as indicated by the radio compass.

Doc was gazing through another instrument. The instrument was built in the bottom of the dirigible. It threw out ultraviolet rays. The rays pierced the artificial cloud, permitted a clear view of the jungle beneath. The bronze man was showing interest in what he saw, for the jungle was well worth inspecting.

It seemed impossible that men afoot could even have penetrated it. For miles and miles, it looked as if it were so dense that a land party would have found it necessary to cut its way through, a foot at a time.

Once in a while there would be a pile of stone, surmounted by vines and brush. These were all that remained of long-forgotten cities. The country was one that would hold exceptional interest for an archaeologist, seeking to trace the history of the past.

Monk and Ham paid silent tribute to those who had courage enough to dare the country afoot and with canoes. Dangerous beasts, deadly snakes and poisonous plants filled the jungle. The rivers were equally dangerous.

Propellers on the dirigible were muted. The air stream thrown out behind them was picked up in wide funnels and so distributed that the sound they made was hardly more than that of a drugstore fan. At the height they were flying, the sound could not be heard on the ground.

It had been hours since they had seen human habitation of any kind. Yet they knew there were humans in the jungle. Explorers who had penetrated part way into the Green Hell and had been lucky enough to return, had written at length of the tribes they had found.

Without exception, they had said the natives were bloodthirsty and untrustworthy. Some members of those exploration parties had been slain treacherously. Others had been forced to fight their way out, battling for days before reaching safety.

The jungle itself was a fierce enough enemy. Coupled with its dark-skinned inhabitants, it was not a foe to be tackled without ample provisions and arms.

Doc's aids did not worry. The dirigible took them in an hour a distance that would have required days on foot. And even if through some mischance they lost the dirigible, they still had confidence Doc would see them through, some way.

The only thing they worried about was Johnny. Now that they were getting closer and closer to their goal, that worry mounted. None liked to speculate on just what they would find. They didn't even want to think of it; but they couldn't help themselves.

Doc turned suddenly, abandoning his inspection of the country below. They were nearing a large cleared space.

"Stop the motors," he said crisply. "We have reached our destination."

RENNY's jaw dropped. Dumbly he pointed to the radio indicator. It was still pointing straight ahead. The needle held fast, did not waver in the least.

Doc's expression did not change. Instead, he pointed to what appeared to be a watch that he held in his hand. The watch was on the same order as the radio indicator, but much smaller. It had only one small hand. That hand was spinning furiously.

"Our friend Hugo Parks thought to deceive us," the bronze man said.

"B-but how?" stammered Renny.

"There were indicators on the parachutes in the plane also," Doc said quietly. "Those indicators were of a different type. This dial shows that the parachutes are beneath us. Parks and the girl undoubtedly left the plane here."

A pleased grin crossed Ham's face. He had wondered if Parks might not try a trick. And the lawyer had expected that Doc would know if such an attempt was made to lead them on a false trail.

Monk was dancing about excitedly. "What are we waiting for, daggonit?" he piped. "Let's go. We got to find Johnny."

"It would be best if we descended after dark. We may be able to accomplish more if it is not known we are here," Doc said.

Monk ducked his head. Doc always was a step ahead of him, he admitted. And much as the chemist wanted to come to immediate grips with whatever dangers threatened, he had to concede that Doc was right. With difficulty, he restrained his impatience.

"We have preparations to make," Doc reminded.

Those preparations helped to pass the time. From a storeroom in the bag of the dirigible itself, parts of a gyroplane were taken out.

Doc and his aids assembled the giro rapidly. The plane was not large, but it would carry as many as three men, although not for a great distance. And it was a true giro—one of the few in the world. It would actually rise straight up, and could land vertically. The huge blades of the giro had sufficient power, also, to hold the ship motionless in the air.

For jungle country such as they intended to explore, it should prove invaluable. Only a small space was needed for either landing or taking off.

The dirigible floated easily and motionlessly. A single propeller was used at intervals to keep it steady; otherwise, its motors were silent.

The bronze man and his aids did not know the cloud that concealed the dirigible was attracting attention. But then, they did not know that Sleek Norton had learned they still lived.

SLEEK NORTON grinned when the cloud was called to his attention. It was the only cloud in the sky. Later in the day there would be more, but that would be when the usual afternoon showers arrived.

Messengers were dispatched from Norton's hide-out to intercept the party guiding Hugo Parks and the girl.

Still later, another group left the camp. A white man was in command of this group. He had definite instructions from Sleek Norton. The man chuckled when he received those instructions. Sleek Norton certainly was a smart boss, he told himself.

Then Norton himself roused into activity. There was much preparing of weapons.

Unaware of the reception being prepared, Monk, Ham and Renny were involved in a very serious procedure.

One man, it had been reluctantly conceded, should stay with the dirigible. Besides, the Autogiro hardly could take more than three at a time, and none wanted to waste minutes making a second trip.

For some time, a three-handed matching game had been in progress. The odd man, it was agreed, should remain behind. With uncanny skill—or knowledge of how the others would probably react—the three turned the coins as if they knew which side should come up. Time after time they either all three had "heads," or all three "tails."

Renny became disgusted. He hurled his penny far out from the dirigible.

"You two work too well as a team," he declared severely. "I might as well stay aboard and be done with it."

"You don't mean that we were giving signals, do you, Renny?" Monk asked innocently.

"Well, perhaps you wouldn't call them signals," Renny said bitterly. "But it was strange that each time your left eyebrow went down, you and Ham both had tails; and that when you wiggled your right eyebrow, you both had heads."

IT was decided that both Chemistry and Habeas Corpus should remain aboard with Renny. Neither Monk nor Ham liked this, but agreed they could return for their pets later if they decided they wanted their help.

Chemistry was again busy, playing his familiar game with Habeas Corpus. And, although the pig had been victimized a hundred times, he never failed to leap up and vainly chase the ape.

Monk and Ham armed themselves with their mercy pistols. The first trip would be one of exploration only, but there was no telling what they would run into.

Doc spent a good twenty minutes in his laboratory. He put article after article in the emergency kit he carried strapped about his body.

That emergency kit was always the bronze man's ace in the hole. Its contents varied from time to time as he replaced things he believed might come in handy in connection with whatever task he was on. This time it probably had as odd an assortment as he had ever carried.

The jungle hid its secrets well, and there were so many things that could happen.

Doc himself took the controls as the Autogiro was lowered through the opening in the bottom of the dirigible, just after dusk. It was the same opening that had been used for the plane Parks stole.

The dirigible was quite high. It had to be. When the giro was freed, it dropped straight down for several hundred feet before the big fans opened and the motor cut in. Then its speed checked slowly.

Doc had a perfect mental picture of the terrain beneath him. Far to the west were cliffs. These had been so screened by the jungle that it had not been possible to get a clear look at them from above. It would have been possible to get closer, but the bronze man made no effort to do so.

With the watch-appearing instrument in his hand, he was following as near a direct course as he could to the parachutes Parks and the girl had used.

The giro landed easily. Then Monk and Ham understood the reason for Doc's actions.

The bronze man donned goggles. Then he took out a flashlight, pressed it on.

There was no beam of white light. In fact, neither Monk nor Ham could tell any light was coming from the flash at all, although they knew there was.

An infrared beam was being used. Through the goggles, the bronze man could see perfectly without the light giving him away in case anyone was watching.

He searched the ground carefully. And the marks on the hard earth gave a perfect picture to his trained mind. He could see that Parks and the girl had been met by a fairly large party. Prints of shoes told him there had been two white men in the group.

Then the flashlight beam twisted, fell on the discarded parachutes. His low, trilling sound filled the air.

Monk and Ham darted forward. Doc picked up a note that had been attached to one of the parachutes. Doc read it aloud:

"Dear Doc: I comprehend your mental machinations sufficiently to understand you will seek elucidation of my fate. *I am a man who has been dead and will die again.* Go! I am beyond assistance. Do not seek to understand. It is beyond understanding. Johnny."

"What does it mean?" Ham burst out.

Doc did not reply. He seemed deep in thought. He pulled a small magnifying glass from his pocket, dusted the paper with a fine powder. Then he studied the paper through the glass.

"There are fingerprints here. They are the prints of Johnny," he said slowly. "But——"

A harsh voice interrupted. It was hard to tell in the darkness from just what direction it came.

"Doc Savage, you are a brave man—but listen!" the voice snapped. "Leave this country and never return. If you do not, you will never be able to leave at all."

Monk tensed. "Let's go get them," he breathed fiercely.

Doc's hand reached out, restrained him. "Wait," he said quietly.

Ham ignored Monk's outbreak and the words of warning

they had just heard. "You started to say something else, Doc," he breathed softly. "Something about Johnny's fingerprints. What was it?"

"The fingerprints," Doc said, "were not those of a living man."

Chapter X

DISASTER STRIKES

Doc's words had the effect of a stunning blow. Neither Monk nor Ham questioned the bronze man's statement. They understood how Doc had arrived at his conclusion.

Fingerprints made by a living person always show perspiration. This would be particularly true in the jungle, close to the equator. The prints left by Johnny's hand showed no such signs of moisture.

Forgotten for the moment was the menace of the warning voice that had told them to flee. They were brought back to realities abruptly.

"Doc Savage! Time enough has been given," the harsh voice called. "Go!"

A low, muttering animal sound came from Monk. The homely chemist's small eyes were gleaming redly. Not for the first time, he resembled the bull ape Ham accused him of being. His long arms swung unconsciously.

Ham pulled to one side. The dapper lawyer also was tense. Johnny must be dead. All evidence pointed to that conclusion. But the note was more than mysterious. It almost appeared to be a real message from the dead. And such things could not be. Ham wanted to investigate.

A hissing sound came. Then there was a burst of brilliant light. Their hidden foes had fired a Very pistol. The entire clearing was as brilliantly visible as if it had been daylight.

Doc and his aids appeared perfect targets. Without hesitation, Monk and Ham dropped to the ground.

The bronze man alone did not move. He had been anticipating such action by their foes. It was the logical thing for them to do. Safe in the concealment of the jungle, they could mow down their helpless victims with machine guns, without danger to themselves.

Had he been alone, Doc might have attempted to elude

63

the bullets that were sure to come if they disobeyed the warning to flee; would probably have sought to reach the safety of the huge trees and underbrush near by.

But Monk and Ham were with him. It would be impossible for all three to reach safety. One or another would be shot down. True, each man was wearing bulletproof underwear, but the cleverness of the ambush indicated they were dealing with a foe that did not underestimate them. The machine guns undoubtedly would be aimed at their heads.

"We have no choice. We must go," Doc said. His voice was louder than usual. It carried easily to the men hidden in the jungle.

Monk growled fiercely. He was inflamed with the desire to fight, to get his hands on those who opposed them, to take out his rage over Johnny's demise on these men who sought to balk their search. For one of the few times in his life, Monk was tempted to disobey the bronze man.

Then he paused. Doc was speaking again. But this time his voice was so low that only Monk and Ham heard what he was saying. Those hidden in the jungle would not have understood, anyway. Doc was using the ancient language of the Mayans.

"We will be permitted to leave without being molested?" Doc asked loudly.

A harsh chuckle came from the jungle. "Get in your kite and pull out, and we won't fire a shot," came the promise. The speaker's voice indicated he knew some jest, secret to all but himself.

Doc did not appear to notice. He walked to the giro and got in. Monk and Ham followed reluctantly.

The huge blades of the giro picked up speed. The ship lifted slowly, straight up. Above the whir of the giro blades came another sound. It was a girl's scream, shrill and terrified.

"Watch out, Doc Savage! They plan to——" Her voice shut off, as if a hand had been placed over her mouth.

Doc pulled a lever. A big propeller in the front of the giro went into action. The ship appeared almost to leap to one side. It was only a score of feet above the ground.

At the same instant there was a terrific blast. Trees and underbrush leaped into the air. The ground for yards around was torn up as though by heavy shell fire, as buried explosive let loose. More Very lights burst in the air. The giro was not to be seen.

THE first flame of light had attracted Renny's attention. The big engineer was on his belly, his eyes riveted to the infrared telescope.

The artificial cloud wasn't the only concealment the dirigible had now. There were real clouds as well, a big field of them, white and soft. The telescope pierced them without difficulty.

A snarl came from Renny when he saw the giro and the figures of his three friends in the field below. He didn't need a diagram to tell him they had not been the ones to set off the light, and that consequently they must have run into trouble.

He got up, put on a parachute and went to the rail, stood poised there for a moment, tempted to jump.

Then he shook his head. His orders had been explicit. He was to remain aboard the dirigible no matter what happened. Without the airship, eventual departure from the Green Hell district would be more than difficult.

He had just returned to the telescope when the explosion came. Even high in the air, the big ship rocked from the concussion.

Perhaps that was why Renny did not hear faint sounds from above. He was too intent in trying to find out what had happened to Doc and the others.

Monk and Ham wondered for an instant what had happened, even though Doc had warned them what to expect.

The explosion had seemed to be almost in their faces. It took them a moment or so to realize that there had been several distinct explosions. One of the blasts had been of the rocket type. Doc had set it off just a fraction of a second before the attempt was made to kill them.

The giro shot across the clearing almost with the speed of light, shooting up to clear the tree-tops at the opposite side at the last possible moment. It was well out of sight when the Very lights came on.

Doc had seen traces of the hidden explosive, had understood what was to occur, and had warned his aids in Mayan.

Even so, the speed with which things had happened had left them dazed.

"Take the controls," Doc told Monk.

The hairy chemist gulped, and obeyed.

"Return to the dirigible and keep out of sight for the time being," Doc continued. "I will signal you when I want you to return."

Before Monk or Ham had a chance to argue, the bronze man left the giro. He had held it, almost motionless, directly over a big tree. His body landed in that tree with scarcely a sound. Then he vanished.

"Daggonit!" Monk protested. "Here we just get to where it looks like we got some fun, and we got to go back."

"Doc is right," Ham said soberly. "We can't land where we were before without being seen, and it's just as well they think we're either dead or have run away."

Monk muttered to himself. He let the giro rise for a few feet and made a slow circuit, looking in vain for another good spot to come down. But he took care to stay well out of the range of the Very lights.

He wasted a good ten minutes before he obeyed Doc's instructions. Later, he was to wish he hadn't done that.

OTHER sounds followed the faint bump on top of the dirigible, but Renny was too intent on what was going on below him to hear them.

Chemistry got up, walked around sniffing, and even rubbed against the big engineer. The ape was pushed aside.

The top of the dirigible looked as if a swarm of bees had suddenly landed on it. There were a score of dark objects there. Rope ladders were hooked to a catwalk along the top of the airship, then were dropped over the side. Men swarmed down them.

The first warning Renny had was when two men landed almost on top of him.

The two men were slightly off balance. They had blackjacks, but didn't get a chance to use them, for Renny came up off the floor as though he had been on springs.

He had been wanting action, wanting someone on whom to take out the rage that burned in him.

His bony monstrosities of fists lashed out. Those fists could

Guess who's doing his thing on the poster scene?

The mysterious good-guy, tough-guy superhero is the newest, now-est poster going. Here he is in living color — the glistening bronze skin and golden eyes, the energy and daring that'll make any enemy alive wish he were a friend.

Whether you're a high school or college student, or a guy who remembers Doc from way back when, Doc Savage is where it's at. Where it's happening. So get ready for the Age of Savage, with this exciting color poster. Or, get more than one and impress a few friends on their birthdays. Just $2.00 each.

break through solid doors, and they found it easy to smash jaws. The men went over backward with their features greatly altered.

Then many things seemed to happen at once.

Men boiled around Renny from all sides, made a mass attack on Doc's aid.

One of the men landed almost on Habeas Corpus. The pig was still half asleep. His head was banged on the floor. Habeas thought Chemistry was playing again.

The pig snorted angrily, leaped up. He saw a flying figure near the rail of the dirigible. Rage overcame Habeas's habitual caution. His long legs propelled him in a gigantic leap.

In the same moment, a reeling figure plunged into him. Habeas had time only for one startled squeal. Then he was over the side of the dirigible and falling toward the earth, thousands of feet beneath.

Renny was a good fighter. Had he been able to reach a place where he could have gotten his back to a wall, the battle might have lasted much longer. As it was, there was a row of fallen figures around him before two blackjacks hit him at the same time from behind.

The big engineer shook his head, tried to turn around. Men dived at his legs; others caught his powerful arms. He was smashed down by sheer weight of numbers.

Once again a blackjack rose and fell.

Chemistry had seen Habeas Corpus go over the side. For a full minute the big ape clung to ropes where he could look down. Pitiful, crooning sounds came from him.

The ape's eyes were as red as those of Monk when he turned his attention back to the fight. He dived into the mêlée looking almost exactly like the homely chemist.

Chemistry had waited just thirty seconds too long to do Renny any good. He received the undivided attention of the sky pirates. He stood no chance.

Only minutes after the invaders first reached the top of the dirigible, they were in control.

A well-dressed figure came down a rope ladder, surveyed the scene of battle with sardonic eyes. Then Sleek Norton gave crisp orders.

Some of the men went back up the ladders to where a second dirigible loafed overhead. That dirigible had been waiting, hiding in the clouds, until Doc and the others had been seen to descend. Then they had made the attack.

Renny was tied securely. No one paid much attention to Chemistry. He appeared dead to the world.

Then one of the men whose actions showed that he knew what he was about, went to the controls. Motors hummed softly; propellers moved.

A few moments later both dirigibles were underway.

Chapter XI

TOMB OF THE DEAD

EVEN when Monk did start the giro ascending, he moved it up slowly. He adjusted a peculiar pair of night glasses to his little eyes.

"I don't like Doc bein' down there alone," he muttered.

Ham reached over, took the controls. "He's probably safer than I am with you, and much safer than if you were along," the lawyer snapped.

Monk grinned. "I'm built for that jungle work, shyster," he said. "This country ain't no courtroom."

"You'd probably look for the girl," Ham pointed out. "Girls always make more of a monkey out of you than you look like—if that's possible."

Monk merely grunted. He was busy watching Doc. Through the seemingly opaque glasses, he could see a giant form going through the treetops. Doc's body was covered with a chemical solution that fluoresced at night, when viewed through the peculiar binoculars. At great distances, he and his aids could locate each other in the darkness.

"You'd think he was runnin' on a race track," Monk reported. "He——"

"E-e-e-e-e-e-e!"

Monk leaped as if a hat pin had been jabbed into him. "You danged legal burglar," he squeaked. "Stop imitatin' Habeas or I'll pound your chin into the toes of your shoes."

Ham looked as startled as his hairy companion. He opened his mouth to answer.

"E-e-e-e-e-e-e!"

The squeal was lower this time. It was a squeal of fright, of panic. Then a crash of underbrush drifted up to the noiseless giro. Monk jumped up and down.

"It was Habeas!" he bellowed.

"Something's wrong above," Ham snapped. He increased the upward speed of the giro.

"Dang it, let me out of here," Monk piped shrilly. "Somebody's tossed Habeas overboard! I'm going after him!"

"Sit still!" Ham roared. "You can look for your blasted pig later. There's trouble up above. There's got to be. We've got to get up there and help."

Monk gulped. He realized Ham was right. Then he said softly: "Habeas was a swell pal. I'll get the bird who threw him off that dirigible. I'll tear him apart with my hands."

For once, Ham did not respond. The great blades of the giro were grinding at top speed. The fuselage canted at a dangerous angle as they bit into the night air. Ham strained his eyes, tried to catch sight of the big, cigar-shaped bag. There was nothing to be seen.

They shot up into the bottom of the cloud bank—and thought the world had come to an end.

THE whirling blades of the giro sliced through a blanket of small balloons. The balloons had been freed by Sleek Norton's men, and had been left directly in the path the giro would have to take if it tried to return to the dirigible.

The balloons were filled with a suffocating gas.

Monk and Ham had been caught unprepared. They had no time to get out oxygen tablets. In fact, their lungs already had drawn in deep breaths of the deadly gas. They acted instinctively and without hesitation, taking the only course they could to save their lives.

As Monk switched off the power of the giro, they both dived overboard, head-first. They dropped for more than a thousand feet before they pulled the rip cords on their parachutes. They had to get away from the gas, and get away fast.

The jerk of the opening chute spun Ham around like a top. Then he yelled. A hairy figure was plunging down on him with a parachute still unopened.

"Keep away from me, you prehistoric numskull, or you'll knock us both batty!" the lawyer shouted.

An answer came from a hundred feet below. "I ain't anywhere near you," Monk squawked. "You're seein' things!"

In the same instant, the hairy figure shot past Ham, barely

missing him. A moment later another chute billowed out. Ham began to laugh.

"It's Chemistry. He must have got a parachute and bailed out. He couldn't stand being separated from you."

Monk snorted in disgust. "That fool ape." Then he grunted, as if a thought had smacked him in the face. "Swell!" he shouted. "I got an idea. We'll catch up with Doc. I'll put you in your place, too, you animated writ of certiorari."

"You'll probably kill us both," Ham snapped from the swinging shrouds of his chute. "At that, it'll be almost worth sacrificing me to get you out of the way."

Neither mentioned the questions that were troubling them most. There was no use discussing things that couldn't be helped. But both realized the plight they were in.

The dirigible was gone, how or why they did not know. Renny was probably in severe trouble. They had been forced to abandon the giro. Doc was miles away.

Their force was badly split. They were in hostile country, surrounded by enemies and without supplies. And there was still the green death and Johnny's fate to be explained.

Neither appeared to mind. If it hadn't been for thought of Habeas and Johnny, Monk would have been almost happy. He was always happiest when the going was toughest.

THE jungle had completely swallowed Doc Savage. Had it been daylight, little illumination would have reached him, for the towering trees of the old bush of the South American jungle met overhead. Then there was the middle bush and the new bush. It was all but impassable.

On the ground, it would have been necessary to cut a path in many places. Doc went through the leafy branches sixty or seventy feet in the air. He was following the faint scent of smoke. Where there was smoke, there should be human beings.

The jungle was plentifully inhabited. Monkeys chattered high above the bronze man. There were more deadly beasts, also. Gleaming yellow eyes followed the course of the bronze man. The monkeys stopped their chattering suddenly. In the same instant a long shape streaked through the air.

Doc moved as the monkeys quieted. He released his hold, dropped in midair. The plunging shape almost struck him, doubling in the center of its leap to lash out with giant claws. It was one of the feared jungle cats of the South American bush.

Huge as a tiger, it was even more ferocious. It had the agility of a leopard and could tear a man to thin strips. Had its claws caught, Doc would have been mutilated, possibly killed.

The claws did not. Fast as the cat was, Doc was even faster. His two hands shot out, caught the rear legs of the giant cat, and twisted. An almost human shriek came from the cat. Without leverage, it was unable to free itself. With Doc holding on tightly, the two plunged toward the ground.

Branches broke their fall. And when they landed, the jungle cat was on the bottom. All Doc's weight caught the animal in the belly, momentarily stunning it. The bronze man did not pause; he was on his feet instantly, had leaped again for a tree. In a moment he was gone.

The great cat growled throatily, went on in search of easier prey.

For many minutes Doc continued on his way. The smell of smoke grew stronger. Then, abruptly, the trees ended. Cautiously, the bronze man descended to the ground and advanced. It was as if he were entering a vale of silence.

Jungle noises ceased; not a blade of grass rustled, not a thing moved to show anything living was near. There was a queer tension in the air, an atmosphere of gloom.

Strange, saw-toothed blades of grass reached up hungrily. A sweetish odor, as of flowers, filled the nostrils. But there were no flowers.

Doc paused, his keen nose twitching. Then he donned his goggles and flicked on his flashlight. A low, trilling sound filled the air. Doc Savage had learned something about the Green Hell district. It was a detail that apparently had puzzled him. For long moments he was very busy. Then he went on.

A FAINT trail led upward on the opposite side of the cleared space. In the distance, even in the darkness, could be seen the dim bulk of massive cliffs. Lights seemed to flicker there.

With goggles still over his eyes, the bronze man inspected the path with his infrared flashlight. There were faint footsteps visible. The prints appeared recent. Doc moved ahead, but he moved cautiously, stopping frequently. He strained his finely attuned ears to catch the slightest sound. He heard nothing. That was a tribute to his attackers. The onslaught came without an instant's warning.

A heavy-headed spear whizzed through the air. Any other would have been impaled by that spear. Doc heard a faint sound of indrawn breath as the weapon was hurled. He dodged, and the spear merely grazed his neck.

Brown shapes materialized from the underbrush. They appeared from all sides. The bronze man reached for the mercy pistol at his belt, then his hand dropped. He could not use even mercy bullets on those who opposed him.

He was encircled by women!

They were garbed in various kinds of jungle dress that revealed much of their figures.

The women were tall, their faces painted fiercely, their arms muscular. So well were they proportioned, that they appeared to be perfect physical specimens. Some of their features, despite the paint, were beautiful.

But they were not soft. They were veritable amazons— and their intent was warlike.

Doc had no time for extended scrutiny. He had no time to attempt a parley. One of the women barked a sharp order. Spear arms came back.

The bronze man leaped. He went straight upward just as those spears smashed toward him.

Cries of rage pursued him as he raced through the tree-tops. The women sped along beneath him. But even going through the trees, Doc was outdistancing them.

Then the trees ended. The cliffs appeared sharply ahead. More armed women were racing from those cliffs. They were carrying torches and calling back and forth to one another. The tongue they spoke was a strange one.

Doc's gold-flecked eyes sparkled slightly. Few men would have recognized that they were speaking a mixture of Chero-kee and Sioux. Doc did. He knew it was one of the un-explainable mysteries of the ages that the language of North American Indians, in a garbled form, was spoken by tribes in the heart of Brazil. And he was a student of those languages.

"Kill the intruder! He must not be permitted to escape!" came the cries.

An unreasoning frenzy appeared to grip the women. It would be impossible to speak to them in their present mood. And pursuit was drawing closer from behind. Those racing from the cliffs were almost close enough for the rays from their torches to reach the bronze man.

Doc reached in his pocket. His hand made a sweeping motion in the air. Then he walked ahead, slowly and confidently.

The onrushing women did not pause. They swept by him so close that some almost touched him. But none appeared to see him.

Then the two groups of women met. There was excited chattering as each group accused the other of permitting the bronze man to escape. The women who had come from the cliffs were rubbing their eyes. Those eyes were faintly irritating. They did not realize that, for several moments, they had been almost blind!

Doc had thrown a powder in the air, which, combined with the smoke from the torches, made it impossible to see anything close at hand. During those moments, Doc had passed them.

The bronze man broke into a swift run, turning so that he could skirt the cliffs and survey the land.

Then he stopped running. He stopped very abruptly as the ground vanished from beneath his feet. The next moment he was falling—falling——

The opening through which Doc plunged had once been secure. It evidently had been weakened by the tropical rains. And the sides were of stone. The bronze man was thrown forward, his head striking those stones as he fell.

Doc did not move for some time after he regained consciousness. It was his habit to remain quiet, to get his thoughts in order if there were things he did not know.

And he did not know how long he had been out. It probably had been several hours. The fact that he was not a captive made it reasonable to presume that the women who had been hunting him had not noticed the opening through which he had fallen.

Through the thin space above him, he could see that it was still dark. There was no noise about him. But there was a strange odor, a faintly sweet odor.

The air in the underground cavern was surprisingly cold and dry. Apparently it had other openings through which the air circulated.

Doc's powerful fingers came up, touched the large bump on his forehead. Then he used the fingers of both hands, massaging the bump with tremendous strength. The bump disappeared.

Doc got to his feet.

The goggles he had worn had been broken when he fell. He obtained another set from the emergency kit around his waist. The kit he wore was so cushioned that it took far more than an ordinary spill to break the objects it contained.

The flashlight flicked on, and Doc's low, trilling sound filled the cavern—for he was in a cavern of the dead.

The vault was a large one fully fifty feet wide and extending for as far as the light would carry in either direction. The walls had been hacked away to form niche after niche, resembling those in the catacombs of Rome.

In each niche rested a body.

For the most part, the bodies were those of women. Occasionally, there was that of a man. The men's forms were scrawny and puny compared to those of the women. It was easy to see why the women apparently were the rulers.

Dust covered some of the bodies, sometimes a half inch thick. Those bodies had been there for a long time. Yet each was in perfect condition. Except that they were green.

The burial cavern contained only bodies of those who had fallen victims to the green death.

Swiftly, Doc went up and down the walls, inspecting each body briefly. Then he came to a slab separated from the rest. The body on the slab was that of a man. But this man had been exceptionally tall, although thin. His clothing hung from his body in ill-fitting folds. Glasses were still on his nose.

Hugo Parks had not lied—at least, about one thing. The body was that of William Harper Littlejohn, known as "Johnny" to his friends.

And he *had* been a victim of the green death.

Chapter XII

MONK TUMBLES

MONK's parachute ripped on the high branches of a tree. He made the rest of his downward trip without any deterring agent. He landed on the part of his anatomy normally used for sitting down and said, "Oomph!" He said it loudly. Ham and Chemistry landed near by.

Monk squinted at the sky. "Wind took us back some," he observed. "Habeas must have landed somewhere near here."

Ham started to comment, then changed his mind. Monk had thought a lot of the odd-appearing porker.

"I'm goin' to look for Habeas," Monk said. His voice choked a little. "At least he deserves a decent burial."

Monk unstrapped the chute harness, started to beat about through the underbrush. Suddenly, he bellowed in delight. "He's alive!" he squalled. "It don't seem possible!"

The homely chemist charged ahead into the underbrush. Ham could dimly see the form of a pig rushing to meet him. But it was no friendly reunion. The pig lashed out with sharp teeth!

Monk squealed in surprise. The pig tried to dive through his legs. But the chemist was built too close to the ground. Bellowing in astonishment, Monk was carried on the animal's back through the underbrush. Ham laughed so hard he had to sit down.

The animal Monk had encountered was not Habeas. It was a strange breed of South American peccary. And it was very angry.

Chemistry made the mistake of trying to go to Monk's aid. The ape jumped back in surprise as the peccary lashed at him with its teeth. Monk fell off then and the peccary scampered into the bush.

"Monk," Ham said sarcastically, "I always knew a pig would be your downfall."

Monk glowered at him, rubbed his hands where sharp briars had scratched them. Then, surprisingly, he grinned. He began to shed his clothes.

"Your own downfall is on the way, shyster," he piped. He walked over to Chemistry, began to bark in guttural tones. Chemistry seemed to nod in understanding.

Ham's jaw dropped; an uneasy expression crossed his face. He didn't think Monk understood any language he didn't know.

"What's going on, you hairy mistake?" he demanded. "What've you got up your sleeve?"

Monk didn't reply. He strode about making mysterious motions with his hands. He took off more clothing. Soon he was down to his underwear. He took a tube of brownish paste from one of his pockets, began to smear it over his body.

"You better do the same," he advised Ham solemnly. "Otherwise, we'll leave you here alone." He began to talk gibberish again to Chemistry.

"What in——" Ham snapped. "Have you gone all the way off your nut?"

Monk surveyed him owlishly, eyes dancing. "I've waited years for this moment, you dandified law book," he growled. "Too long have you referred to me as a breed of ape. Right now we apes have the upper hand. We're all going to become apes. That's the only way we can travel."

SERIOUS for a moment, Monk explained that travel on the ground was hazardous. They didn't know where their foes were, but they might be near. Also, it was difficult to move through the underbrush without making noise.

If they wanted to investigate at all, the safest way was to travel overhead.

Then Monk grinned again. He laughed aloud and his head seemed to entirely disappear behind his huge, wide-open mouth.

"Come on, shyster," he gloated. "You ain't in a courtroom now. You gotta take to the trees." Once more he appeared to speak to Chemistry.

Ham's face wore a strangely baffled expression. For once,

he knew, Monk had him where he wanted him. The chemist's logic was good.

"But you're not kidding me about talking to Chemistry," he snapped. "That's just your jungle idea of humor."

Slowly, reluctantly, the dapper lawyer shed his elegant clothes. With obvious distaste, he also smeared his body with brown paste. Then the three took to the trees.

Only Chemistry could travel with the ease Doc Savage had shown, although Monk was nearly as nimble as the ape. Ham found the going definitely tough. Time after time he saved himself from a fall only by a desperate scramble. Monk's face was crimson with suppressed laughter.

"Laugh, blast you!" Ham said bitterly. "This is no hardship for you. You're built for it. We'll probably never get shoes on you again."

The first part of Ham's statement was quite accurate. Monk looked and acted pretty much like Chemistry. And Ham was definitely not built for the work.

"You should 'a' stuck to a law practice," Monk growled. "Doc made a mistake takin' you outta a courtroom."

Chemistry gamboled on ahead. His guttural barking drifted back to Monk and Ham. Monk was forced to slow his pace, because of the lawyer. Twice he had to help Ham back up from a precarious position after Ham had missed a hand hold and plunged downward.

But Ham was game. He stopped complaining. Perhaps he didn't want to give Monk the chance for further ribbing.

Monk suddenly stumbled into a furry body. "Dang it, Chemistry!" he muttered. "Can't you keep out of the—*yow!*"

The last word came sharply. It wasn't Chemistry he'd stumbled over. The trees suddenly seemed filled with counterparts of the pet ape. Monk remembered that it was in a South American jungle that they had found Chemistry. No zoologist had ever seen a similar specimen. But the South American jungle has more unexplored area than any other part of the world.

There were two dozen "Chemistrys" here. And they seemed to object greatly to the presence of Monk and Ham. Their leader leaped upon the chemist. Two others lunged at Ham.

Monk suddenly forgot his caution and the necessity for being quiet. "Chemistry! Chemistry!" he squealed. Desperately, he and Ham held to tree limbs.

There was a great threshing in the trees. The real Chemistry hurtled down through branches. He jabbered at a great rate. He made an oration that even Ham agreed, later, was worthy of any lawyer.

The other apes appeared uncertain. They glanced at one another. Chemistry gave a high-pitched squeal. Dramatically he leaped forward, put one hairy arm about Monk's neck.

The leader of the apes let Monk go. He scratched his fuzzy head, then barked an order. A moment later the apes were gone.

"Saved!" breathed Ham. "Saved—because Chemistry introduced them to a fellow ape!"

Tears of mirth rolled down the lawyer's face. Monk might have scored first, but Ham believed that at least he was even. And Monk was speechless. Chemistry's actions had been too plain. There was nothing for him to say.

For some time they moved on, making as little noise as possible. They had no definite destination in view, but were trying to take the same general direction as that followed by Doc.

Then Chemistry began to act in a peculiar manner. He jumped up and down, pointing with one hairy arm. Monk lifted his head, his broad nostrils dilated.

"Smoke!" he said. "Chemistry's discovered something."

Silently the two followed the ape. The smell of smoke grew stronger. It was wood smoke, apparently from a campfire. The trees grew thicker. Monk called Chemistry back and took the lead himself. Ham struggled along behind.

They were a queer-looking trio. Monk, looking like some huge, barrel-chested simian, moved with the greatest caution; but occasionally branches snapped under his weight. Each time he stopped and listened carefully. Soon faint voices drifted through the night. Most of them were the voices of men. But one was that of a girl.

And there was one voice that rose above the others—Hugo Parks's.

"They don't call me Brains for nothing," the large-headed

man gloated. "We know Doc Savage got into the cliff tribe. That ends him. We already got one of his men, and the other two are in the jungle. We'll pick them up in the morning. Everything is jake."

Monk moved forward slowly. He saw a small clearing. Hugo Parks sprawled on the ground, looking into the campfire. Gloria Delpane sat beside him.

"And tomorrow you'll take me to the one I want to see?" she asked softly. "You know that everything is all right?"

Hugo Parks grinned. He patted a portable short-wave set beside him. "This helps me to know a lot of things," he said. "Yeah, everything is all right. Why, even the green death——" He broke off.

Gloria fell silent. There were half a dozen armed gangsters around the fire. They drew nearer the blaze when Brains mentioned the green death.

Monk crawled farther out on the limb of a tree overhead. He tried to catch everything Hugo Parks was saying. Parks mopped perspiration from his huge head. He even seemed awed with himself. His voice rose to a harsh cackle.

"The green death will work for us," he gloated. "Even the dead will have their uses. The big guy has got all the answers now. We're all goin' to be millionaires."

Hugo Parks's voice sank. "It's got the natives ga-ga," he said. "They've lived with it all their lives. But now they are plenty scared." He paused. "They have reason to be," he added in a whisper. "It's uncanny. I never believed in mumbo-jumbo before. But this here's——"

A loud snap interrupted him. There was a crash and a shout. Ham twisted around. Monk's body was hurtling down through the air. He had crawled too far out on the limb of the tree, and it had broken under his weight.

Monk went down howling.

It was going to be a fight. Whatever happened, Monk would be happy, for he loved to fight. The hairy chemist landed on a big-framed gangster. Monk's fists balled into bone-crushing weapons. He swung them right and left.

"It's an ape!" Hugo Parks shrieked. "Get it! Kill it!"

One of the gunmen grabbed a Thompson submachine gun. He had the weapon at his shoulder, ready to pull the trigger, when Parks knocked it aside. The big-headed man was grinning.

"No, it ain't an ape," he shouted. "It's just that guy of Doc Savage's who looks like an ape. He's fallen right into our hands. Take him alive."

Taking Monk alive proved to be a more difficult job than Parks had figured on. It became even tougher a moment later, for Ham and Chemistry arrived. They came straight down, landing in the middle of the fighting throng.

The gangsters became a bit confused. The campfire embers scattered. Monk bellowed in the pleasure of fighting. First one gunman went down, then another. Suddenly, Gloria Delpane screamed.

"A-a-a-*Thing*," she shrieked. "It's a——"

A vague, white form bounded into the clearing. In the scattered reflection of the campfire embers, it seemed to have no definite shape. Hugo Parks looked at it once, and his eyes seemed ready to pop out of his head. He grabbed the machine gun he had first knocked aside.

"Hold it or I'll blast you!" he bellowed. "I want you alive, but I ain't goin' to fight no ghosts."

Monk dived at Hugo's legs. Hugo went over on his back, the machine gun spraying the sky harmlessly with lead.

Ham spun to meet the menace of the white charging "Thing." He lunged at it; but it eluded his grasp, then turned on him. Sharp teeth nipped at Ham's legs. One of the gangsters laughed. The laugh was a little hysterical, but it was still a laugh.

The white attacker came apart slowly. The tangled folds of a parachute tore and ripped. Through them wriggled the scrawny body of Habeas Corpus, Monk's pet pig. The porker nuzzled against Ham, as if apologizing for having bitten him.

"Goshamighty!" Monk stuttered. "It's Habeas!" He dived toward the lean pig, grabbed it in his arms, the fight forgotten for the instant.

That was a mistake. Hugo Parks leaped to his feet. Monk was gurgling happily. It had been only a few days before that he had constructed a parachute for Habeas. He had fastened it on like a saddle on a horse. Then he had forgotten about it.

Hugo Parks swung the butt end of the machine gun. It

caught Monk in the back of the head just as three gunmen bore Ham to the ground, slugging him viciously with black-jacks.

Chemistry raced for Habeas, picked the pig up under one arm and stared about belligerently. No one paid any attention to him. They were all too busy tying up Monk and Ham.

Parks bent to the short-wave set, tapped out code. Then he listened for an answer. He smiled grimly.

"Okay, boys," he grated. "We take these guys to head-quarters. Doc Savage's hash is being settled for keeps this time."

The throb of drums sounded faintly in the distance. Hugo Parks's grin grew broader as he heard the sound.

Chapter XIII

RAIDERS ATTACK

THE drums were beating in the cliff city. They were being pounded by small, scrawny-appearing men who gazed about nervously.

There was much activity all about them. The giant bronze man who had been seen to enter, had not been found. Patrols of the amazons were searching every inch of the canyon and cliffs. The men were not permitted to join in the search. They were not considered fit for such work. Tending the campfires, cooking and other menial jobs was their lot.

Zehi hunted alone. She always preferred to hunt by herself. She was a tall woman, standing an easy six feet, with broad shoulders and powerful arms. She swung a heavy ax and gazed at the men contemptuously.

Zehi had been one of those who had surprised the bronze man in the forest. Her eyes lighted with admiration as she recalled how he had looked, then she glanced about hastily, as though others could read her thoughts. It was not well to let the Princess Molah know that they had any feeling except scorn for men.

Her bare feet padded noiselessly as she went through winding hallways in the cliff. Her course led downward steadily. Zehi paid little attention to her surroundings. An archaeologist would have been in his glory.

Elaborate paintings were on smooth stone walls. Those paintings traced the history of the tribe; told of the time, hundreds of years before, when the Incas had fled before the Spaniards, when some had disappeared into the jungle never to reappear.

Bright-colored stones had been used for intricate decoration in some of the paintings, but Zehi ignored these, also. After all, few now could read them—and what did it matter? Only Pterlodin pretended to know what they meant.

Zehi's lips curled as she thought of Pterlodin. He was a man, a medicine man, but he certainly didn't have the looks of the bronze giant.

The ax swung viciously in Zehi's large hand. Pterlodin! A fine medicine man he was! With evil white men camped not far away, with hostile tribes around them, waiting like vultures for a chance to attack, Pterlodin had disappeared.

And he was the only one who knew how to control the green death!

ZEHI's breath came in sharply as she thought of the green death. Her pace increased, almost became a run.

Of course, there was one place it would be possible to hide with little fear of detection. The cavern of death, the place where the victims of the green death were kept.

That was another silly idea of Pterlodin's, she thought scornfully. Why should those bodies be kept from the flames or the sacrificial pit any more than any others?

A long, sloping runway took her down beneath the level of the earth. She grabbed a torch from a wall as she ran, and shivered suddenly. Pterlodin had warned against visiting the cavern of death. It was taboo. But Pterlodin was missing —and the bronze stranger must be hiding there.

Zehi turned a corner, reached a heavy door. Holding the torch in her mouth, she tugged until she had freed a large bar. Then she tried to scream, a purely feminine scream. She was not very successful. The torch in her mouth was something of a handicap.

Powerful bronze hands caught her arms, took the ax from her as if she had been an infant. Then she was pulled inside the cavern of death, and the door closed behind her.

"There are things I would like to know, that I believe you can tell me," Doc Savage said quietly. He spoke in the mixture of Cherokee and Sioux that was the language of the cliff city.

Zehi's eyes bulged. Weird lights illuminated the cavern of the dead. The bronze stranger appeared even larger at close quarters than he had at a distance.

But strangest of all were the many articles laid out on one of the slabs. Zehi had never seen such things before, some bright and shiny, others transparent and seemingly holding liquids. Then she had no time to notice more. The bronze man began to ask questions. Zehi did not want to answer. She felt she could not help herself. The stranger's eyes exerted a hypnotic effect.

It was Doc who caught the first hint of danger. He leaped to the huge door, bolted it from the inside.

Then Zehi also heard running feet. They stopped just outside the door. Axes beat on the door. Angry voices were raised threateningly. Zehi shrank back, her face paling as she heard the words.

"Someone must have seen you seize me," she breathed. "They will kill you. You cannot escape."

Strangely, Zehi did not seem to want Doc Savage to be killed.

OTHERS had a different idea.

A war party was slinking through the jungle a few miles away. The warriors were painted grotesquely. They had been whipped to murderous, frenzied bravery by experts. One of the experts danced at the head of the cordon. He was a little man. Two antelope horns protruded from a skull cap. A string of human teeth dangled from his neck. He had an ugly, hawk-beaked face.

Zehi would have been greatly surprised could she have seen him. He was Pterlodin, the missing medicine man, the only man who knew the secret of the green death!

Pterlodin had great plans for himself. He chanted weirdly as he danced at the head of the war party. His beady eyes gleamed fanatically. He was like a madman with a single fixation—a fixation about to be accomplished.

Pterlodin did not seem to consider himself treacherous in leading an attack against his own tribe. He appeared proud.

For Pterlodin had ambition. He was medicine man to the tribe of women. But a medicine man was still a man, something tolerated rather than revered. Pterlodin resented his scrawny body. But he was going to be king, master of those who had ruled for so long. Pterlodin licked thin lips as he danced at the head of the savage tribe.

He had enlisted the aid of the deadly Herdotan warriors, the most feared tribe of the Matto Grosso. He would rule the

Herdotan as well as the Amazons. The Herdotan could have the women for their wives.

Pterlodin's eyes snapped as he visualized the groveling surrender of proud Princess Molah. Pterlodin would rule the Matto Grosso. That was as it should be. Did not Pterlodin understand the green death? Could he not control it?

The madman raced up and down the slinking column. One white man stumbled along with the savages. The white man was bound. His face was bearded, haggard. The eyes were red-rimmed and bloodshot. He was a small man, clad in the remnants of leather puttees and khaki flying togs. Pterlodin snarled and spat as he passed the white man.

The name of this one Pterlodin had not troubled to ascertain. He had merely acted as an interpreter between the savages and the one named Norton—Norton, who had promised Pterlodin what support he needed. Pterlodin spat again. Norton would die also when he was through with him. All white men were to die.

Pterlodin had been canny. He had not told Norton all he knew. He was smart enough to know that Norton would double-cross him. And Pterlodin hated white men even more than he hated the women who had ruled him.

Several miles away, Monk and Ham twisted uneasily as they heard the sound of the drums. There was an ominous tone about them, a note of doom. They wished they knew what they meant.

"If you hadn't gone back to your ancestral state, we wouldn't be in this jam," Ham snapped. "You're dumber as an ape than you are as a chemist."

"Aw, shut up!" Monk growled. "Where you're goin' they got too many lawyers already. They'll probably throw you out and I won't have to listen to you."

"If you ever listen to me again it'll be while I'm lecturing in a museum," Ham muttered—"on evolution!"

At Sleek Norton's headquarters, Renny also twisted in his bonds. He thought he knew what those drums were all about. Beads of perspiration were dropping from the engineer's face.

He had learned much in the short time that had elapsed

since he had been surprised and overpowered on the dirigible. Too much for his peace of mind.

Renny was tied about as securely as it was possible to bind a man, pinioned firmly to a chair. He knew that Sleek Norton had dispatched a tribe of fierce warriors to attack the cliff city. He knew Doc Savage was there. And he knew Sleek Norton.

Sleek Norton had been the brains behind New York rackets and crime for many years. He had been public enemy No. 1 long before the Feds began to number them. But when they did get Norton's number, Sleek had begun to travel for his health. Even while away, he still gave orders to lesser thugs who took the rap, or went on one-way rides.

Now Sleek was tarrying in the Green Hell section of the jungle. That meant the stake was plenty big. Sleek was not noted for matching pennies.

Just what the stake was, Renny was not sure. He knew the green death was grimly mixed into it. And he knew that Norton considered the extermination of Doc Savage as necessary to his success, even though Sleek had first thought he needed Doc to help him.

That much, Sleek had given away by accident. But just what Sleek Norton's evil purpose was, Renny had not been able to learn.

It had been sufficiently important for Sleek to send Hugo Parks to New York, to lure Doc to the jungle. Then it had been important enough for Sleek to take drastic steps to prevent Doc from arriving.

But Doc had not been stopped. Doc was there—in immediate danger of his life. And his aids were separated, helpless. One of them was a victim of the green death.

Frantically, Renny twisted at his bonds, used more than ordinary strength in a futile attempt to loosen them. He had just seen the fastidious form of Sleek Norton enter one of the dirigibles moored at the edge of the clearing. One of the airships was Doc's. The other belonged to Sleek. Renny twisted mightily. If he could get free, get to that other dirigible, he might be able to help Doc.

Norton came out of the dirigible, strode to a knot of gangsters. They stood before one of the modern portable houses Sleek had brought into the jungle. He even had his own electric plant, had refrigerators and fans. Something mighty big had made Sleek set up that permanent headquarters.

Renny gave a great heave. He didn't care how many men he had to fight. He had to help Doc. Suddenly he felt a sense of freedom. The ropes did not give. But the modern, tube-steel chair back groaned, then snapped.

Renny jerked erect. Behind them, the dandified figure of Sleek Norton stepped softly. Sleek's eyes narrowed just a little. His lips smiled cruelly. With one smooth gesture he pulled a heavy automatic from his shoulder holster, slammed the butt down on Renny's skull.

The big engineer collapsed. He did not hear the sudden change in the tempo of the drums, did not hear the clamor that drifted over the jungle—a clamor of rage, then of panic.

Chapter XIV

A PRINCESS COMMANDS

Doc Savage was having woman trouble. The woman was
Zehi, and she was obdurate. She did not understand. Doc had
no difficulty in speaking her language. It was only that her
lack of knowledge made it difficult for her to comprehend
why she should put the white tablet on her tongue. It
seemed like a trick.

Zehi was more than anxious that Doc Savage escape. It
should be easy for him to go out the same way he had come
in. Zehi even showed him where there was a long notched
pole he could use for a ladder.

But the bronze giant insisted she put the white tablet on
her tongue. It was necessary, he told her, to save her life.
Finally Zehi shrugged, obeyed instructions. It was difficult to
argue with this man. He might even be a god and not a man
at all.

Thick fumes swirled about them in the cavern of the dead.
The fumes were pierced by a strange light. Zehi had never
seen that kind of light before. It didn't flicker like a torch. It
was a straight, pale beam.

She sniffed the fumes that were being pumped over the
door of the vaultlike cavern. She explained to Doc in the
language of the village. She called it by its native name.
But her description was that of a vaporized form of curare,
the dreaded poison of the jungle. It paralyzed the lungs, then
the entire body, before death ensued.

Doc Savage nodded. He already had identified the swirling
vapor. That was one reason for his speed. He leaned over the
greenish form of Johnny. His hands were swift. The bronze
man did not reply to Zehi's explanations. He asked her
questions, asked about the wailing chant that was rising outside the huge door.

Zehi answered excitedly. She told him it was the sacrificial chant. He was to be the sacrifice. "Flee!" she pleaded. "You can get out the way you came in. I will show you how."

Doc Savage did not reply. He handed her another oxygen lozenge to combat the effect of the poison vapors. Zehi took it absently, followed the bronze man as he went rapidly from one niche to another. Doc hovered for a moment over each greenish body. Then he returned to Johnny.

Beside the body of the archaeologist were two large cases. The amazons had visited Johnny's last camp, had recovered his equipment cases and entombed them with him. Doc opened one. He took out a compact short-wave receiver, clamped the earphones to his head. Doc knew that Hugo Parks used short wave for communication.

Suddenly, he straightened, spoke to Zehi.

"The village is to be attacked," Doc said simply. "Your entire tribe is in danger of being killed. Tell me just what is going to happen to me?"

Zehi spoke swiftly. Doc continued inspecting Johnny's equipment cases. Again Zehi urged him to flee.

The bronze man did not even answer. He had come to find Johnny. He had done so. But he could not leave as long as there was a chance he could do anything for the archaeologist. And he could not leave for another reason, now.

The village was to be attacked. Savages were going to seek to kill and capture the women. Doc's entire life had been dedicated to fighting injustice. He could not stand by idly and see the savages triumphant.

"You will go into the sacrificial fire," Zehi panted. "Nothing can halt it once the chant of sacrifice has started. You will die."

Zehi coughed suddenly. Doc pressed another oxygen tablet upon her. It was the last one he had. He took a deep breath as he exhausted the tablet in his mouth. Then he breathed no more. He had a remarkable ability to go long minutes without breathing. But there is a limit, even to the most remarkable physique.

Doc Savage leaned briefly over the form of Johnny. His lips were close to Johnny's head, as if he were saying farewell. Then two things happened almost simultaneously.

Doc Savage staggered. His hands caught at his throat. Then the door of the cavern of the dead crashed open.

Women warriors stood there, tense, spears poised. The bronze form of Doc Savage lay inertly on the floor.

"The poison has gotten him!" Zehi gasped. "He—he gave me something to save me."

Then Zehi blushed. She lowered her eyes, wondered if she also would be sacrificed for fraternizing with a man, even if he did act like a god.

LIGHT breeze cleared the cavern of the poison vapors. The women warriors backed aside, opened a path. Had Doc Savage's eyes not been closed, he would have witnessed an entrance that might well have impressed even him.

Beauty is a relative thing. But no matter what standards might have been used as comparison, it was definitely beauty that walked into the cavern of the dead. The plume in the woman's hair was an aigrette. It had cost the life of the bird of paradise that had given it. The finely molded features below the burnished-copper brow of its wearer could well have been a model for any nation's coinage.

The eyes were widely spaced, cool and direct. The lips needed no cosmetics. They were red and full, with a mouth that was generous but firm. The symmetry of the woman's body was apparent. She walked with an easy, straight-shouldered sway. Zehi prostrated herself before the amazon.

"Princess Molah!" she moaned. "If he dies, give me also to the tongues of the eternal fire."

Princess Molah paid no attention to the prostrate Zehi. She had found it expedient, upon occasion, to overlook any interest some of her sex showed in men. The princess stooped over the bronze man. Her lips pursed in an expression of surprise.

Unconsciously, Princess Molah's hand went to her white aigrette. She wanted to be sure it was on straight. She had never seen a man like Doc Savage, and she was still a woman, even though a warrior.

Then stern lines of discipline tightened about her mouth. The tradition of centuries could not be overcome.

"Carry him to the sacrificial fire," she ordered. Her voice was low, a husky, powerful contralto.

Scrawny men scrambled into the cavern. They were cowed

males, ever seeming ready to dodge. Eight of them seized the limp form of the bronze man, carried him out onto a wide enclosure on the cliff.

Princess Molah followed. There was a peculiar expression upon her face. It was both of bitterness and of doubt. She followed the prostrate bronze man to an altar beside a yawning crevice. Fires raged within the pit. Actually, the crevice was merely the escapage of nautral gas that had become ignited.

There is much oil in South America. Also there is gas. But to the amazons it was a never-ending sacred fire. It had been put there by the spirits that guarded the tribe. Things had not gone well of late. The spirits must be appeased.

Princess Molah sighed as the bronze man was placed upon the blood-flaked altar beside the pit. She moved mechanically as the chanting of the tribeswomen increased in tempo. She picked up a curved knife, faced the fire a moment.

Then she turned over Doc Savage. Slowly, the knife began to fall.

No one was watching the door to the cavern of the dead. Perhaps it would have been taken as an omen if a savage guard had been watching there.

Outside, a life was being taken. In the dark confines of the cavern, a dead man began to move. The greenish tint on the face of William Harper Littlejohn began to pale. The archaeologist stirred slightly. The eyelids flickered. A gusty snore ended in a weak expression.

"A chimerical phantasmagoria of a deranged cerebrum," the gaunt Johnny wheezed. It was not unusual that Johnny's first words should be the longest he could think of.

Then Johnny sat up with a snap. It might be a mere dread, but Johnny's lips phrased one word that was burned into his consciousness, one that bridged from the subconscious to the conscious.

"Doc," he blurted, "how in the devil did——"

Johnny began to move. He had no idea how he had come to be where he was, had no idea Doc could have gotten to him. But he knew a post-hypnotic impulse when he encountered one.

Somehow, Doc Savage had given him explicit instructions.

Johnny had no time to wonder what had happened, how he seemed to be alive when he thought he was dead. He hardly cared.

The gaunt archaeologist sprang to the two equipment boxes that were beside the slab on which he lay. Johnny had never seen the route he was taking. But he knew exactly what to do. He carried the equipment cases with him.

When Johnny saw the bronze man, he disobeyed instructions. He saw more than did Doc.

Johnny began to shout in Mayan. It was a language few men in the civilized world understood. The language of ancient Maya had become known to Doc and his aids many years before; behind that knowledge was the secret of the limitless wealth of the bronze man, the wealth he used to war on injustice.

Princess Molah whirled, the knife in her hand. The words of Johnny had not gone unrecognized in the cliff city. "The language of the lost!" the princess gasped.

Then several things occurred with great rapidity.

Doc Savage turned slightly. One cabled hand flicked out and a powder fell into the sacred fire. The blaze leaped a hundred feet or more into the air. Thick green smoke began to fill the enclosure on the cliff. A shout of fear and amazement went up from the women. Doc had expected that; but he had not expected the other cries that rent the air.

The advance guard of the Herdotan warriors had gotten down on the ladders. Doc Savage had not been able to see them from where he lay. The form of Princess Molah was in the way. Johnny had seen the marauders climbing down like spiders. That was why he had cried out.

But the yells had drowned out his words. Doc had not understood what Johnny said. The bronze man leaped to his feet as spears whistled through the air. The amazons showed they were real warriors. They leaped upon the attacking Herdotan fighters who had gotten onto the floor beneath the cliff.

The rest of the attackers never reached their destination. The burst of flame that Doc had intended to use for another effect, had leaped high on the beetle brow of the cliff side above. It had swept the rope ladders of the Herdotan tribesmen like a blowtorch turned on a spider web.

Men screamed as they let go their holds. The dry hemp burned like a fuse, licked upward, cutting off escape or attack. Doc Savage had no intention of bringing death, even to those bent upon his murder—but it could not be avoided.

Those who were still above looked down upon the village from the safety of the plateau. Angry curses came from their lips. Suddenly a hush fell. One man screamed, clapped his hands over his eyes. He began to make very fast tracks down the path in the jungle.

The scrawny face of Pterlodin, the medicine man, wore a look of disbelief. His little eyes grew larger, seemed trying to pop from his ugly head.

What he saw was the dead come to life. He noticed green puffs of smoke rise from the barren ground. In the smoke women appeared, women with spears ready for attack. They looked like women that he, Pterlodin, knew to be dead.

Pterlodin shuddered. Then another thought seemed to come to him, one that brought a more active fear to his face. He scurried into the jungle, raced toward the headquarters of Sleek Norton. Pterlodin thought he knew what the next step of the racketeer would be.

In the cliff city, Johnny was very busy. He worked over a little black box, following the directions Doc had given him. The women were highly excited, for the bronze man had caused the eternal fires themselves to leap. It was very strange.

The fires had leaped up and beaten their enemy. Now the women looked about them in awe. They saw figures that must be dead, victims of the green death. The figures walked in the smoke made by the bronze man.

Doc had not expected the arrival of the Herdotan tribesmen so quickly. He had discovered in the cavern of the dead that Johnny, using a telescopic lens, had made motion pictures of the amazons during his exploration work. He had merely directed Johnny to use his portable projector to throw the pictures on smoke Doc would cause.

The smoke had been green. The features of those in the

pictures were not plain, and it seemed they were victims of the green death returned to life.

Doc's strategy had been to impress the women sufficiently, so they would permit him to aid in beating off the attack he knew was coming. That had not proved necessary. But Johnny had carried out his instructions.

Doc barked orders at Johnny then. They were in English, and the women did not understand that language. Johnny turned on a portable fan he used to clear foul air from caverns he wished to investigate in his geological investigations. The greenish smoke dissipated.

"Doc," Johnny bawled, "how did you get me back to life? What's been going on?" He was so excited that, for once, he forgot to use big words.

Johnny was full of questions, but the bronze man had no time to answer. The women converged upon him. They appeared grateful, yet there was something else besides gratitude in their faces. There was grim determination.

Princess Molah went from one to the other of her warriors. She spoke in such a low tone that Doc could not overhear her. Other squads of female soldiers quickly seized Johnny. They bound him tightly, threw him into a dwelling carved from the solid rock of the cliff.

Princess Molah's voice came clear and strong. "You will not be harmed, bronze man. Go quietly. The word of Princess Molah is your bond."

Doc was prodded along at the points of spears. He could have broken away, might even have gotten Johnny free. But there were several things he wished to learn before he quitted the cliff city. And he knew the first attack by Sleek Norton would not be the last.

He wanted to find out what other vulnerable points the city had. But the bronze man did not realize what was in store for him. His first inkling of that came from Johnny.

The gaunt geologist had scrambled to his feet. He stuck his head out of a barred window. One of the women passed him, and Johnny demanded to know what was going on. The woman was Zehi. Her face was very sad. It was probably her own sadness that made her confide in the bronze man's companion. She was quite bitter about it.

Johnny burst out into a loud guffaw of laughter. He almost fell over. Laughter was not known to the amazons. They turned, curiously. Johnny roared again.

"An unrequited act of superamalgamated hospitality," he howled.

"You're tagged, Doc," he shouted. "The big girl likes you. We're neither of us ever to leave here, they tell me. You're the only man the number one girl ever found fit to be her husband."

Johnny could not help his laughter. Doc almost always had a similar effect on women. But none other had ever taken such drastic measures about it.

Chapter XV

INTO THE ARMS OF DEATH

THE scene in Sleek Norton's camp was sort of a jungle pastoral. The bigshot gangster was going in for agriculture. He was having quite a good time about it. He had started out with a construction job, ordering the Indians to dig a deep cellar. It wasn't exactly a cellar—it just looked like one.

Then he sent a long file of Indians out into the night. They shuddered when they went. Sleek Norton gave them their choice of doing what he told them—or of digesting a lead-nosed bullet. The Indians were just as much afraid of that as they were of the green death. So they went.

When they returned, a long file of them, each bore a huge basket on his head. It was filled with grass. At each trip the cellarlike pit grew more full of grass. Sleek Norton chuckled louder and rubbed his hands.

"This is excellent," he gloated. "Doc Savage is dead by now. So we'll give his three playmates the green death. And that fool ape as well."

Chemistry had bitten Sleek soon after Hugo Parks had reached the main camp with his prisoners and Gloria Delpane. Brains Parks paced behind Norton. He rubbed his huge head with a bandanna handkerchief.

"We'll have the world by the tail," he purred. "We——"

Norton whirled on him. "*We*, hell!" he snorted. "You'll be in clover just so long as you do what I tell you. Don't forget that—or start getting ideas of your own."

Gloria Delpane materialized from the shadows. Her eyes were doubtful. "You told me——" she started to say.

Parks smiled. He tried to make it an inviting smile. "Now don't worry, Gloria. It will all turn out all right. And don't let this well-dressed dude frighten you."

"Cut it, cut it!" Norton growled. "You can have the dame, though you wouldn't if you had any brains."

Monk and Ham had been gagged. Their incessant ribbing had begun to get on Sleek Norton's nerves.

But gagging them hadn't solved the problem entirely. Someone had found Ham's immaculate attire in the jungle. The fastidious lawyer had hung his clothes on a tree limb but now they lay on the ground.

Monk was methodically wiping his feet on his companion's spotless morning coat. Each time he did, he looked innocently at Ham. The lawyer apparently would die of apoplexy long before the green death got him.

Sleek Norton saw it and screamed. He had had all of Monk and Ham that he could stand. He kicked the clothing away, then planted a heel in Monk's ribs.

"Take the gags off them," he rapped. "I want to hear them holler when the death gets 'em. They'll be dead soon after sunup."

Ham's first words were, "Will you please kick this imitation ape once again for me? My feet are tied."

Sleek Norton snorted. He told the gangsters to shove the four into the pit. A shudder ran through the gangsters as they moved to obey.

A SUDDEN commotion in the jungle interrupted them. Frantic cries of fear bubbled from savage lips. The frightened tribesmen who had attacked the cliff city tumbled into the light. Ahead of them, they shoved the haggard, unkempt man who acted as Norton's interpreter.

Pterlodin had intended to kill that one if the attack on the village had been successful. That would have cut Norton off from contact with the Herdotan warriors. Norton could not speak the language. But the attack had been unsuccessful.

A cry of delight came from Gloria Delpane as she saw the unkempt man. She tried to rush forward. Hugo Parks slammed her back roughly. For a moment, it appeared the haggard man would attack him. Then his shoulders shrugged resignedly.

One of the returning natives babbled a tale of fear. Norton made the haggard man translate. The native told of the great blaze of fire. Norton whirled. His lips worked with rage.

"You, you yellow-livered——"

The native kept right on babbling. He told of the big bronze man. Norton's expression changed from one of rage to fear.

"I told you that you couldn't lick Doc Savage," Ham jibed triumphantly.

Sleek Norton whirled. "Into the pit with them," he bellowed.

The gangsters leaped to do Sleek's bidding. Big-fisted Renny was the first to go. "Good luck, guys," he gritted. "See you in Green Hell!"

"I was goin' to save that village," Sleek Norton blustered. "There might be treasure there. But now it goes off the map like a pinch of dust. I got the whole cliff mined. We'll blow it all to hell."

Monk was the last of Doc's aids to go. When Chemistry saw Ham tossed into the mass of green leaves, the ape rolled in by himself. Wherever Ham went was good enough for Chemistry.

Monk was doing his best to scratch Habeas Corpus's back. "Scram, pig," he squalled. "Try and find Doc. There's no use in you dyin', too."

Sleek Norton stalked over to Gloria Delpane. The girl still was dazed from the blow Hugo Parks had given her. She seemed to be trying to talk to the haggard man. Norton prevented that. He lashed her to a tree, gagged her.

"It isn't that I don't trust you, baby," he purred. "But I think you'll do nicely this way."

THERE were two guards outside the cavelike dwelling in which Doc Savage was held prisoner by the amazons. That made it easier. One of the guards thought she heard the other call to her. She went along the lip of the cliff to answer. Behind her, a silent figure slipped out through the door.

By the time the guard decided her ears had played her a trick, the figure that had left the prison had disappeared.

The bronze man wished to do a bit of reconnoitering. He slipped noiselessly through the darkness, turned a corner, then flattened against a wall. Footsteps, strange-sounding footsteps, were approaching. They suddenly seemed to start to run. Doc did not move. His gold-flecked eyes flashed strangely. The cold nose of Habeas nuzzled against his leg.

Monk had told Habeas to find Doc. And Habeas had used his nose. With the agility of a mountain goat, the shoat had picked his way along a path too narrow for a man.

Doc picked up the porker. There was nothing unusual about his appearance. Habeas looked as he always did. Then the bronze man sprinkled a powder on Habeas's hairy back. A message immediately flouresced in the darkness. In Monk's handwriting, he saw the following warning:

If you are in the cliff city, get out immediately. The entire city is to be blown up. It is mined underneath. So long, Doc. We're getting the green death.

Doc whipped quickly from his hiding place. In another minute he was outside the cagelike cliff house that held Johnny. "Return to Monk," the bronze man told Habeas. The porker hesitated, squealed protestingly, but obeyed.

Doc whispered questions to Johnny.

"There's an underground passageway," Johnny replied. "Zehi told me about it a few minutes ago. She wants us to get away. She said the women are afraid of it. It's some sort of superstition."

Doc tried the door to Johnny's prison. It was constructed of some kind of metal. It did not budge. The bronze man wasted no time trying to force the door by ordinary means. He stood back a few feet, hurled a tiny vial.

A searing, blinding flame climbed into the air. Doc hurled another vial. Concentrated Thermit compound burned the metal door as if it had been paper. The white-hot flame glared brilliantly on the cliffside. Cries of alarm rose in the night as the women guards raced madly forward.

Doc Savage unbound Johnny. The two raced along the edge of the dwellings. But the village had suddenly come to life; every girl warrior in the place rushed to intercept them. The controlled voice of Princess Molah rang out.

"Kill him!" she ordered. "He is better dead than as an enemy!"

It seemed Doc had impressed her more than enough.

Spears whistled through the air. Johnny pointed toward a ragged hole in a wall at one end of the village. "That must be it," he grunted. "That's where Zehi said it was."

Doc raced along. He could not stop to argue. He knew the women would prevent him from going into a sacred passageway, even if he could convince them that they were in danger. But if the cliff was mined, that underground passageway was the most likely place for explosives to be hidden.

THE warriors saw their direction. Guttural commands rang out. A line of fifty women backed toward the entrance to the sacred passageway. Others began to converge on Doc and Johnny.

Suddenly, the lanky geologist found he was running all alone. Doc had disappeared. The warriors were almost upon Johnny. They didn't bother hurling spears at him. They were confident he could not get away.

Doc's voice rang out. "This way, Johnny! Quick!"

The voice came from Johnny's left. He turned obediently, began to race toward the sound. In an instant he found himself enveloped in a cloud of thick smoke. He felt powerful hands upon his shoulders. He was spun about, headed in the opposite direction.

Doc's voice continued to issue from the other side of the open space. "This way, Johnny! Right up the cliff!"

More puffs of smoke rode from the clearing. Johnny heard the faint clicking of his portable projector. He hoped the batteries were still good.

They were. Two vague figures suddenly glowed luminously in the puffs of smoke. They might have been the forms of Doc and Johnny. They seemed to walk right up the side of the cliff.

The women screamed with rage. Spear after spear was hurled through the vague, smokelike figures. The women were expert marksmen; scarcely a spear missed its intended spot.

Meanwhile, Doc and Johnny raced toward the entrance to the sacred passageway. A yell went up behind them. Johnny looked over his shoulder, began to run faster. "They've discovered it's a trick," he shouted. "They're busting up the projector."

More accurately, a few of them were breaking the projector. The rest were pounding over the hard-baked ground to head off Doc and Johnny.

The two were scarcely a dozen yards ahead when they plunged into the ragged hole. The women pulled up short. They did not attempt to hurl spears into the black maw of the tunnel. They spoke in low tones among themselves. The tall figure of Princess Molah strode in among them. She paused a moment, then spoke.

"You have chosen your own end, bronze man," she said. "I can do no more for you."

Her voice seemed tinged with regret. She reached forward, pulled a hidden lever. A stone door slid down from the roof and cut off retreat.

THE passageway was roughly hewn through native rock, the floor slimy. Doc thrust a pencil of light ahead with his flash, saw that the corridor narrowed. A sluggish underground stream crossed the floor. The walls were smooth and wet. Small animals, resembling rats, scurried ahead of them.

As the metal door clanged behind him, Johnny whirled. Yellow eyes glared balefully at him. A jungle cat let out a screech.

"Run, Doc! Through the stream!" Johnny yelled.

One of the small animals, frightened by the scream of the jungle cat, plunged into the underground river. Commotion churned the water; it became red with blood, and Johnny drew back, amazed.

"A submarine disturbance of teratogenic proportions," the skinny archaeologist muttered.

"Piranha," Doc said. "They could make a skeleton of a horse in a dozen minutes. These streams are full of them."

Again the jungle cat yowled in the darkness of the tunnel.

"Come on!" Doc said. He flung a tiny capsule in the water as he stepped forward. There was a dull explosion and a small geyser of water shot up.

"Minor explosive," the bronze man explained. "It will act like a depth bomb. It will not kill the fish, but they will be stunned for a few moments."

Doc and Renny plunged through the stream. It was waist deep.

In a moment, they were on the other side, still moving forward. The character of the underground passageway changed. Where before it had been only of slimy rock, now there were bushes of some type. Occasionally there was a small, stunted tree.

A peculiar hissing sound came from the bushes. Johnny leaped to one side as an armlike tentacle reached out for him.

Doc leaped to Johnny's rescue. His light was on the coiling thing that was reaching for the archaeologist. He didn't see the second coil that swept out. The coil was bigger than a man's arm. It was the coil of a giant boa constrictor. It grabbed Doc firmly about the waist, pulled him from his feet.

Chapter XVI

BETWEEN TWO FIRES

SLEEK NORTON was displeased. The gangsters who walked single file behind him were more than usually quiet. Once, when Sleek Norton had been angered, he had pulled out all the toenails of one of his henchmen. The man had made a mistake on a job he was doing.

Sleek was more than normally displeased this time. The gangsters thought it was probably a good thing that Pterlodin hadn't come back; that is, a good thing for the medicine man. Most of the gangsters would have enjoyed seeing Pterlodin's toenails pulled out. And Pterlodin had been so confident he could capture the cliff city.

Norton growled loudly, mostly to himself, as he strode at the head of the column. "There's a mile-long tunnel," he rasped. "Halfway up, I got my firing switches. I'll blow the other half of that tunnel and the whole cliff all to hell."

He strode on in silence for a moment. "We'll make the whole thing a pile of dust," he added. "It'll bury them women and Doc Savage so deep a stream dredge couldn't find them."

One of the quietest listeners Norton had was about fifty feet from him. Norton didn't see this member of his audience. He probably would have thought about toenails if he had.

There was panic in the cruel, painted face of Pterlodin. His antelope horns waggled in terror as he crept along in the bush. Pterlodin had picked up quite a bit of English. He did not understand all that Norton said, but he did understand enough to make him shiver with fear. He might want to conquer the village, but he did not want the cliff city destroyed.

Pterlodin grew more panic-stricken. Suddenly the muscles of his face tightened. It might have been remorse or conscience; at any rate, he apparently came to a decision.

He tore through the bush at an unbelievable rate of speed. Soon, he could no longer hear Sleek Norton at all. He sped to the plateau above the cliff village.

The medicine man had a vine rope of his own hidden there. Making one end secure, he let it down over the bulging cliff, slid quickly and silently to the floor of the village. He knew he would not be welcomed by a friendly reception committee. He knew he had to do a lot of fast explaining.

But Pterlodin was not quite prepared for the bedlam he found. The women warriors were rushing back and forth. They talked loudly to each other. It took the medicine man only a moment or two to realize what had happened. The bronze one and his friend had escaped through the sacred tunnel.

A frown appeared on Pterlodin's face at mention of Doc's aid. Then the frown was replaced by a crafty smile. He was so pleased he began talking to himself.

"What Norton really wants," he said, "is the death of the bronze one. Perhaps I can accomplish two things with a single effort."

The medicine man walked straight into a crowd of female warriors. They towered above him. A howl of rage went up when they saw the fugitive. Half a dozen of them rushed him with outthrust spears. Pterlodin began to tremble. He fell to the ground and groveled, begged to be taken to Princess Molah at once.

PTERLODIN did not need to pretend fear. He was very much terrified. The women might become impatient, run a spear through his chest. True, Pterlodin had been their medicine man. But he was still a man. They had more tolerated than feared him.

But even worse than that, Pterlodin knew Sleek Norton and his men would not be long in reaching their underground explosives. The time element had escaped him until now. He blubbered and crawled along the ground to the princess. She stopped him with a spear thrust into the flesh of his back.

Pterlodin lay flat, talked into the ground. "Princess Molah," he moaned, "I bring you word of your enemies.

I have not been against you, as it seems. I have really been protecting your very lives."

"How, worm?" the princess snapped. "Speak quickly before I impale you as you deserve."

"Spare me, princess," Pterlodin wept. "I come to warn you of the bronze man's trickery. Even now he is about to destroy our city with fire that comes from the earth. He has no doubt killed the sacred serpents and will destroy us all."

The crack about the serpents was just a guess. But it made a roaring mob of the women. Not only were the sacred boas worshiped, but those remarks showed that the women feared something dreadful would happen if the serpents died. They were paying a high compliment to Doc Savage when they showed they believed he might be able to conquer the boas.

They rushed to the stone door of the sacred passage. Intricate counterweights pulled it open. Much as they feared to enter the passageway, the women feared more not to. The Princess's voice rose above the rest.

"If the bronze man has survived the serpents, kill him!" she screamed. "His body must be burned to ashes. The bronze one is an evil spirit!"

The warriors rushed down the sacred passageway. The entire village turned out. They crowded one behind the other. Long planks were passed down to the leaders, placed across the stream that harbored the deadly piranha. The women pushed forward. Some held torches; more held spears and arrows tipped with deadly poison.

SLEEK NORTON reached the outer entrance to the tunnel-like passageway even before Pterlodin had reached the cliff city. The entrance was merely a jagged hole in the hillside, and was well concealed by underbrush. Sleek halted his gangsters for a moment.

Norton had learned originally of the passageway from Pterlodin, but the terrors of snakes, deadly fish and poisonous reptiles that the medicine man had told about, had halted the racketeer from following the tunnel all the way to the cliff city.

"What do we do, boss?" one of the gangsters queried.

"You go along with me," Norton snapped. "There are some animals in there. Shoot anything that moves. Don't wait to find out what it is."

Electric torches lighted up the tunnel as Sleek went cautiously forward. Water dripped from the roof above. The place was dank, slimy. More than one gangster shuddered in apprehension, for the tunnel had a forbidding, tomblike atmosphere. It held a musty smell, as if it had been dead a thousand years.

Suddenly Sleek Norton stopped, mouthed a curse. Far ahead came the roar of female voices. It was the cry of a pack ready for the kill. Sleek Norton didn't know Doc Savage and Johnny were near the center of the tunnel. But he did know the amazons were coming down from the other end. So he made a quick decision.

"Run," he snapped. "We got to get to those TNT switches before the dames get there."

Norton threw caution to the blackness behind him. He raced up the slimy floor. His gangsters pressed close behind him, Tommy guns ready for instant action.

For once, Doc Savage had encountered muscles that were far greater than his own. The boa constrictor was a good two feet in circumference at the middle. Its slimy coils completely encircled the bronze man.

Doc struggled, trying to bring his arms up in order to reach into the equipment vest he wore. Corded muscles on his neck stuck out like cables. The snake merely shifted, tightened its coils. The more the bronze man struggled, the tighter the boa closed its grip.

Johnny only spoke once. That was when the first boa they had met seized him. "Extraordinary tonicity of the co-arctation muscles," he muttered. Haring delivered himself of that, Johnny fought in silence.

Doc Savage also battled noiselessly. His hands were free only to the wrist. He tried every jujitsu hold that was available with such a short purchase. He attempted to contract his great chest suddenly, strove vainly to wriggle sufficiently clear to get at his equipment vest.

The great slimy serpent merely tightened the stifling coils. Bones and muscles strained. Then the bronze man went limp.

His head hung languidly to one side. The flake-gold eyes were stilled. A faint gasp came from his lips. That was all.

The boa constrictor was hungry, for he had not been fed in a long time. No doubt the amazons kept the snake in a half-famished state. That assured them he would attack any attempted intruder—or any hapless prisoner they decided to sacrifice to the serpent god. The prisoner, of course, would believe he was escaping.

The boa relaxed its coils slightly, but not entirely. It merely lessened its grip about the part of the meal to be swallowed first. Doc's head was turned toward the maw. A small antelope had been the snake's largest single meal heretofore.

But a boa can disjoint its jaws to receive almost any size meal. The limit of distension is miraculous. The jaws opened wide enough for Doc's head and shoulders. A boa constrictor does not chew its food; it doesn't even bite it. It merely swallows it whole and lets the powerful gastric juices do the rest.

It was unfortunate for this particular boa that it had been so hungry. Had it not been, it might have continued crushing for quite some time before attempting to swallow its meal.

Doc Savage had depended upon that when he let himself go limp. If the snake were sufficiently famished, it would begin to swallow at once. The boa had to let Doc's arms go in order to reach for the legs. Doc had never been unconscious an instant.

The second the big coils shifted, Doc's fingers were in his equipment vest. A hypodermic needle was whipped out of a pocket. It jabbed through to the inner lining of the big snake's stomach. The reptile began to relax. Doc jabbed the hypodermic a second time.

But minutes were being lost. Doc's present position was a sound-proofed one. He didn't hear the commotion at either end of the passageway. Not until he wriggled free. Then the bronze man heard the uproar, saw the women racing down from the upper end.

At that moment one of Norton's gangsters shot at something in the lower end of the tunnel.

Doc Savage whipped toward the boa that held Johnny. The skinny geologist was unconscious. Doc jabbed with the hypo, pulled at the giant coils with his cabled hands. Another hypodermic appeared in his fist. He jabbed this one into the veins at Johnny's neck. Johnny's eyelids flickered.

"Astounding phenomena of resuscitation," he muttered.

Johnny's return to normalcy was amazingly fast. He did not have the powers of resuscitation that Doc had. But the compound the bronze man had shot into his system restored his strength immediately.

Doc Savage stood erect. The plunging women were almost upon them. They shrieked that Doc had killed the sacred serpents. Doc and Johnny could quickly have outdistanced the female warriors. But Sleek Norton's men were coming from the other way.

It was not impossible that Doc and Johnny might trick them, might get past into the outer air. The confusion when the forces of the women met the gangsters would be terrific.

But Doc knew Sleek must have explosives somewhere in the sacred passageway. And he did not want to expose the women to the deadly fire of the Tommy guns carried by the gangsters.

A weird, trilling sound filled the cavern. It made the amazons falter, hesitate. It was a ghostly sort of sound in the underground cavern.

Doc snapped quick orders. "Pick up your snake, Johnny," he said. "Follow me."

Doc hefted the huge boa that had attacked him. The women gasped. It seemed impossible that one man could carry such a giant reptile. The boa that had attacked Johnny was much smaller. But even that one was no mean burden for a man of strength. Johnny staggered slightly, but he ran, close on the heels of the bronze man.

Doc Savage was not using his flashlight. The faint flicker from the women's torches behind was all the light he had. But that was enough for eyes trained to see in almost total darkness. Doc found the firing switches set by Sleek Norton. They were of a modern type used for remote detonation of blasting. The coils were high-tension, built to withstand any kind of weather.

Doc's first move was to rip up the wiring. He gave it a tug and a hundred feet or more came loose from the wall of the tunnel. Doc rolled it into a ball, hurled it into a crevice. It would take some time to repair the damage, even if Sleek Norton did reach the firing boxes.

At that moment the women rounded the turn in the tunnel. Doc whirled toward them. In the same motion, he hurled two small glass capsules over his shoulder. It was a mere flick of his fingers, but the capsules sailed more than two hundred feet back down the corridor. A dense fog suddenly blocked the tunnel.

Sleek Norton ran into the fog. It confused him for a moment. He stopped. He had a hunch Doc Savage was involved in that fog, and he didn't want to go on until he could see much more clearly.

Doc whirled toward the onrushing women. He was careful to keep the snake between them. He spoke rapidly in the language of the tribe. And as he spoke. he hung the snake across the passageway. He used fine wire attached to small suction cups. He looked like a side-show snake charmer about to do a trick.

"Your sacred snake is not dead," he said quietly. "But if you advance farther, he will be. Do as I say, and he will be revived."

Princess Molah stepped out in front of her warriors. "It is a trick," she snapped. "Seize the bronze one!"

At that moment, Sleek Norton broke through the fog. "Guns!" he roared. "We've got Doc Savage. Let him have it."

The bronze man moved quickly. He stepped back, one hand darting toward the hanging serpent. His fingers gave a tiny jab. The huge reptile began to writhe slightly; it was definitely alive.

A shout went up from the women. They began to prostrate themselves before the sacred serpent. Doc backed farther, dropped a tiny bomb. Thick, acrid smoke billowed up behind him.

The bronze man's first thought had been for the safety of the women. He did not want them to run into the murderous guns of Sleek Norton and his gang. He had known they would not cross the path of their sacred serpent when they found it alive.

Doc turned to face Sleek Norton. The gangsters were grinning broadly. On all sides were the gunmen. Their Tommy guns were leveled at Doc and Johnny.

"Trigger 'em, boys!" Sleek rasped.

Chapter XVII

CRIMSON WATERS

Doc Savage's arms were at his sides. His flake-gold eyes surveyed the gangsters without emotion. The gunmen grinned cruelly. This was meat and drink to them. They seemed to want to enjoy it as long as possible.

The bronze man raised his arms, just as most any man would do in a stick-up. The instinctive gesture brought a laugh from Sleek Norton. But only briefly.

Doc's arms came up much faster than a man's arms would usually raise. They went up with a purposeful gesture. A faint, whirring sound came then.

Sleek Norton never was quite sure what happened. All he could be certain of was that every flashlight in his mob went out. Those that weren't on at the time were found to be useless. Thin wires attached to a high-frequency generator Doc carried overloaded those flashlights, burned out the bulbs.

"Shoot, boys!" Doc's voice came in the darkness. "Get it over with!"

The gangsters cursed and blasted. The underground passageway became a bedlam of crashing sound. It had been a reckless thing for the gangsters to do. Doc was not where they had heard the voice. In the blackness, their senses of direction left them. Doc had used ventriloquism.

Slugs ricocheted on the rock walls of the cavern. Gunmen screamed as they were felled by their own bullets. Others thought Doc was shooting, and excitedly returned that imaginary fire.

Sleek Norton was smarter than his henchmen. That was why he was a big-shot gangster. As soon as the lights went out, Sleek vacated quickly. He knew too much about Doc Savage to fight him in the dark. Besides, Sleek had other plans. He hadn't believed he would meet Doc Savage in the tunnel. But Sleek was a careful man. That was why he had grown as old as he had. He intended to grow a whole lot older.

Doc Savage and Johnny picked their way down the tunnel. It was very quiet. Johnny was full of questions he hadn't had time to ask the bronze man.

"How'd you get me back to life, Doc?" he demanded. "Was I really dead?"

Johnny was like a man who had been in a delirium. He could not tell what he might have dreamed, or what part of the dream might have really happened.

"No time for questions now," the bronze man said. "We escaped that trap too easily. I believe we are expected."

Johnny fell silent, followed Doc over the rough floor of the tunnel, keeping one hand on the bronze man's back. Even then, Johnny stumbled frequently. Doc's remarkable vision enabled him to step around or over every obstacle.

Finally they saw the glittering lights at the entrance. There was no question but that they were expected. Sleek Norton and two or three surviving gangsters were in plain sight. All had Tommy guns and were peering into the passageway.

The mouth of the tunnel was broad. Just before the passage emerged into the open, it spread out fanwise. There were three different exits. It was as if roaring water once might have coursed down the tunnel, and had created a series of deltas at the bottom.

Doc and Johnny turned to the right-hand passage. It seemed that Sleek and his gang were watching the wrong exit.

"Their backs are toward us," Johnny whispered. "Maybe if we run, we can make it."

The bronze man did a peculiar thing. He turned Johnny about, told him to go down the center exit. That would bring him right out where Johnny could see Sleek and his gangsters were watching.

Johnny bit his lip. It was not like Doc to sacrifice one of his own aids. But Johnny knew, somehow, that Doc must have some plan. "Exceedingly correct, Doc," he whispered, and went down into the face of the gangsters' guns he could see.

Doc passed quietly down the passageway they had both started through.

WHEN the shooting started, Johnny found out why Doc had sent him down the center passageway. Doc yelled in Mayan, told Johnny to fight his way through the jungle, to find the camp where Monk and Ham were held.

Doc plunged into a battle that had Tommy guns against him.

Sleek Norton had expected to catch both the men. He had arranged a clever set of mirrors at the mouth of the tunnel. In glittering light, the gangsters could not be seen. It appeared that he and his men were watching the center outlet. In reality, they were watching the one on the right.

Doc whipped anaesthetic bombs at his foes. Gangsters sighed and went to sleep. There was a sporadic outburst of shots. That was all—or almost all.

Sleek Norton yelled at Hugo Parks. Sleek had seen Johnny start down the other exit. Hugo and Sleek both had instruments that looked like fire extinguishers. Parks lit out after the geologist.

The gang leader took the greatest chance of his life. He held his breath, walked right into the impenetrable cloud of anaesthetic gas. Doc Savage was in the center of that cloud. Norton didn't actually touch the bronze man. He stopped, listened. He heard Doc's footsteps, light as they were. There was just a *swish* in the darkness. A pungent odor filled the air.

Doc whirled, started toward Norton. Norton ran. Just then others of the surviving gangsters poured out of the tunnel. Those who had not shot themselves or each other were kill-crazy. They slammed slugs toward the bronze man. Doc vanished in the tree-tops.

Sleek Norton laughed shrilly. He used sign language to give orders to one of the Indians he had brought along. The Indian grinned, leaped into the trees with a grace that approached that of the bronze man.

Norton laughed again.

At that moment, a file of Herdotan tribesmen threshed out of the jungle. They shoved the bound figure of Johnny ahead of them. He had run almost into their arms.

"We'll give him an easy death," Norton gloated. "Doc will take it the hard way."

DOC SAVAGE had not expected the treat Sleek Norton had prepared for him. But his keen nose told him instantly what had happened. He did not go far before trouble arrived.

Ferocious jungle cats ringed him in. Cats screeched in the night from afar. They raced through the jungle toward Doc as steel filings fly to a magnet. Doc streaked through the trees.

One jungle cat he could have eluded. He might have given successful combat to two or three. But actually a dozen of the huge beasts were leaping after him.

Doc raced on through the trees. He flung himself tirelessly from limb to limb. Just as effortlessly, the great cats pursued. More came from the dense jungle beyond. Those cats would follow Doc until they caught him.

Sleek Norton had concocted a chemical that smelled like blood to a carnivore. Carried on the humid air, it drew every predatory animal in the jungle. Doc could take off his clothes, but it would do no good. Sleek had sprayed the chemical over his skin and hair as well.

Two great cats sprang at the bronze man from each side. Doc dropped like a plummet a dozen feet. Other cats reared up from the ground. They growled throatily, bared long white fangs.

Then the bronze man put all his strength in a final burst of speed. One great cat was gaining, was rushing through the trees at a faster pace than Doc Savage. Water gurgled faintly ahead.

Behind him, a solitary figure followed. It was the Herdotan fighter who had been put on the trail by Sleek Norton. He grinned in anticipation. His face showed he knew it was all over now. Thus he hastened his pursuit.

A great cat struck with an ear-piercing screech. The animal stretched to its full length in one final spring. There was a confused blur of action as it landed.

Then the other cats landed. The tree was on the bank of a tropical river. They seemed to come from all directions. There was a whirling mass of fighting fur.

The tree gave way with a grinding crack, plunged into

the slow-moving stream below. Cats and all were carried downward. Water boiled instantly, became blood-red, and crimson extended for many yards, fanned out, drifted with the current. The boiling in the water continued for many moments. There must have been thousands and thousands of voracious piranha there. They were having the feast of their lives.

One of the big cats screeched once. Then his bones were picked as clean as if a vulture had spent a week on them. That is the way piranha work.

The trailing Indian crept up to the bank. The tree which had collapsed was a small one. It didn't extend more than twenty feet into the river. The stream was almost a hundred feet across.

Herdotan warriors knew no man could have gotten six feet through that water, let alone the remaining eighty. As the Indian watched, a piece of Doc Savage's shirt floated to the top.

The Indian grunted with satisfaction. But he was careful and thorough. He went half a mile up the stream, found a log that bridged the water, and went across.

He came back down the other side, scanned the ground for footprints. Then he raised his voice in triumphant announcement. Though the words he spoke were in the jungle dialect, even an observer who did not know the language would have understood the import.

"The bronze one is gone," he shouted. "He is dead!"

Chapter XVIII

CLOUDS THAT PASS

For the first time in hours, Sleek Norton was downright happy. Word brought by the Indian messenger had raised his spirits. His plan had worked. Doc Savage was dead.

Johnny's thin face became even leaner and paler as he heard the Indian's report. The Indian spared no details. For Norton, the words were translated by the man in tattered khaki and leather puttees. Johnny needed no interpreter. He could understand the language easily.

Gloria Delpane was in the room where Johnny was a prisoner at Norton's main camp. Tears came to her eyes as the man in tattered khaki told the story of the bronze man's end. But there was something odd about her tears. It was almost as though she were not weeping for Doc Savage alone, but for another reason.

Johnny got control of himself with an effort. His voice, when he turned to the girl, was harsh, to hide his quite genuine grief.

"Where do you fit in amid this inexorable predicament?" he asked.

"D-Doc Savage must have believed I was responsible at least for some of his trouble," she sobbed.

"Explain," Johnny rapped gruffly. He was not as susceptible to female charms as was Monk, but even Johnny thought this girl beautfiul.

In short sentences, the girl told all that had happened before Johnny came on the scene. She filled in many blanks for him, helped him to understand why Doc and the others had arrived in the jungle, and the reasons behind many actions.

"I—I know they saw me when I fled their office," she concluded soberly. "Then I drugged their coffee on the

117

dirigible, and fled with Hugo Parks. But I did not know that Parks would try to kill them."

"In other words?" Johnny suggested.

The girl sighed. "I was looking for my brother, Scotty Falcorn," she said.

Johnny's eyes widened.

"I suspected the men who came from the jungle would try and see Mr. Savage, so I went to his office. I arrived there just in time to see Hugo Parks running away. He was carrying a shirt. It looked like a shirt I had made for my brother. So I followed."

"Yes?"

"I caught up with Hugo Parks, and he promised to explain, but then ran away. I guess he got to thinking I might return and tell Mr. Savage I had seen him near Mr. Savage's office, so Parks sent men to my room who kidnaped me."

She gulped, as if reliving that scene.

"But I got away, and found Parks's rooms. There I found the shirt, and it was my brother's. I learned Doc Savage was coming here in his dirigible, so I stowed away aboard it."

"And where does Parks come in?"

"He—he found me on the dirigible. He told me that unless I helped him, that my brother would be killed. I—I was afraid not to help. Besides, he assured me that Doc Savage and his men really were my enemies.

"I—I wanted so to find my brother. I was trying to earn money enough in New York to finance a search for him. I had changed my name, and was making good——"

"And did you find him? Was he here?"

Tears started to course down the girl's cheeks again. Wordlessly, she pointed to the other room where the tattered man was still interpreting for Sleek Norton. The gangster seemed to take delight in having details of Doc Savage's demise related again and again.

"The man with the puttees—he—he is my brother," the girl sobbed. "He is Scotty Falcorn."

JOHNNY said nothing. Sympathy was useless. He understood what had happened to Falcorn. The young flier had cracked up in the jungle. He had been seized as a prisoner by the Indians.

They permitted him to live. Possibly they even acted as though he were their ruler. But in reality he was a captive. He would never be permitted to escape.

Similar reports had once been circulated about the flier, Paul Redfern, who had disappeared in the Green Hell district of the Matto Grosso. No one had ever found Redfern, to learn whether the rumors were true or not; but Falcorn certainly was a prisoner.

And the flier could expect no help from Sleek Norton. The racketeer had no intention of taking anyone back to civilization who might tell what really had happened in the jungle.

Johnny's thoughts were confirmed soon enough.

"We're gettin' out of here, and gettin' out at once," he heard Norton snap. "Prepare both dirigibles for flight right away."

Then Norton's voice dropped. He gave other instructions. Hugo Parks cackled loudly, for the orders seemed to meet his enthusiastic agreement.

Gangsters were protesting in faint, frightened voices. Norton overrode their protests roughly. He got out several rubber suits. The suits were airtight. It would be impossible for men to live in them for long in the jungle heat.

That did not worry Norton. He laughed at the panic-stricken protests, then threatened to kill the next man who opened his mouth. That worked. Between positive death and a chance to live, the gangsters decided they would take the chance.

Three of them were clad in the rubber suits. Their faces were very red. Perspiration poured from them.

Cautiously, they approached the pit where Doc's aids had been thrown. There was a faint, sweetish odor about the pit, but the gangsters could not smell that. All they could do was to swelter in the suits they wore.

Fearfully, acting as if any second they expected to be overcome, or perhaps die, the three got down in the pit. Once there, they acted very hurriedly.

It took all three of them to lift Renny's big body and roll it out. The body was stiff and green, with the peculiar mummified appearance that always marked victims of the green death.

Monk and Ham were removed next. Last of all came the body of Chemistry. There had been some shouted argument between the gangsters before they lifted the ape out. They were in favor of leaving his body there.

Sleek Norton ended the argument by stepping out of the house with a machine gun. Sight of the Tommy was sufficient to have his instructions obeyed.

IN the edge of the clearing, an odd-appearing porker with extra long legs and drooping ears, looked on. An observer might almost have believed the pig realized what was taking place.

Habeas Corpus had obeyed Doc; at least, as much as he could. He had returned to the camp where he had last seen Monk and Ham. But he could no longer smell them. All that he smelled was alien and dangerous.

Habeas whimpered softly when he saw the bodies of his friends taken from the pit. He knew they no longer were in a position to help him. Had he thought they were alive, Habeas would have rushed forward to fight with them. But his nose told him differently.

Forlorn and alone, the pig finally took up a hiding place in a clump of brush, and prepared to wait. There was still the bronze man. Habeas had great faith in Doc. He did not know what Norton and the others had been told.

The bodies of the four victims of the green death were taken aboard Doc's dirigible. Sleek Norton had decided he would use the bronze man's airship for himself. Despite all his money, he had been unable to buy one anywhere near as good as that of Doc's.

To Hugo Parks, Norton deigned to explain a little. "Doc Savage is dead; we all know that. But we'll take no chances. We'll keep the bodies aboard for a while, then drop them off, one at a time, from several thousand feet up. That will end danger for all time."

Parks wagged his big head. "And boy, I can hardly wait until we get back to the bright lights!" he exulted. "What we've got this time is a world-beater. We can almost coin money."

Norton grunted. He tried to make it a pessimistic grunt. He failed. He also was wanting to get back to Broadway, and he wasn't going back empty-handed. Under his arm he carried a good-size lead box. Hugo Parks had a similar one. These they placed aboard Doc's dirigible.

A majority of the gunmen were ordered aboard Norton's airship. Norton decided he could get along with a skeleton crew. But he had several gangsters escort Johnny aboard the ship, then lock him in the same storage room Gloria Delpane had used for a hide-out when she stowed away.

More and more of the Herdotan tribesmen appeared meanwhile. The Indians were almost ominously silent. They watched the preparations for departure with unfriendly eyes and ready weapons.

The white men had promised them much. They had promised, among other things, that the beautiful women of the cliff city would be tamed; that the Indians could have as many as they pleased for their wives.

That promise had not been kept. On the contrary, many of the Herdotan warriors were dead, and the cliff city still was in the hands of the amazons.

Norton, through Scotty Falcorn as interpreter, tried to assure the savages that he would be back. He did intend to come back, he told himself. He would undoubtedly, sooner or later, need more of the stuff he was taking from the Green Hell. And he still wanted to visit the cliff city. There must be treasure there. He preferred to have the tribesmen friendly when he returned.

But if they weren't—— He shrugged, motioned to two of his gunmen. His head made a slight motion, and his eyelids dropped.

The gunmen nodded. Unobtrusively, they got two Tommy guns, made sure the magazines were full of shells. Then they filled their pockets with more ammunition. Their movements were sure and unhurried. This was a job they knew how to handle.

The sleek gang leader made a last trip to the cabin he had used as his headquarters. When he returned, he was carrying several bottles. He handled them as though they were very precious. To him, they were; they held the key that was to bring him millions.

At Norton's command, Scotty Falcorn reluctantly told the Indians to help in launching the two dirigibles. The Indians were sullen and reluctant. Only the menace of Tommy guns finally prevailed upon them to obey.

Slowly, the two bags were walked out to where they could lift into the air. Motors roared; propellers started to turn. The Indians let go the ropes and the bags bobbed up. Aboard Norton's dirigible, the two gunmen who had received Sleek's orders went to work.

They had a very pleasant time. Some men enjoy killing others who are helpless. Their Tommy guns made sullen roars. The running savages beneath had little chance. They were picked off as easily as if they had been ducks in a shooting gallery.

Scotty Falcorn did manage to reach the safety of one of the cottages, but the flier felt the hopelessness of certain death. He had escaped the bullets, but perhaps it would have been better not to have run.

Now the Herdotan Indians would kill him, if any survived. Their method was by torture. It was not pretty to watch; it was far more unpleasant to experience.

THE airships rose slowly in the warm air. Had Norton been a more experienced navigator, he might have chosen another time for his take-off.

Johnny felt as near helplessness and defeat as he had ever been. Three of his friends and Chemistry were lying like green mummies on the deck of the dirigible.

Doc, or what was left of him, was alone in the jungle—provided he had not perished. But even Johnny had lost hope this time. He knew what the end must have been.

The big bags circled for altitude for nearly an hour before Norton gave the order to head north. During that time, Johnny kept his face glued to a small porthole which permitted him to look downward. He could see nothing.

Then hope suddenly flared within him. The dirigibles were beginning to make time, now, their motors picking up a steady, monotonous beat.

But behind the dirigible, Johnny saw something that made his heart jump. A small cloud was in the sky. The cloud appeared to be following the dirigibles. For minute after minute, Johnny watched that cloud. Sometimes it seemed to him that it almost caught up with the dirigibles; then he was not so sure.

He was forced to confess that he might be imagining things; that what he thought was a pursuing cloud might really be a series of small ones that the dirigibles were over-hauling. Then Norton appeared in the doorway.

As usual, he was accompanied by two highly efficient-appearing guards. Although Johnny was tied and looked puny in comparison with the rest of Doc's men, the racketeer was taking no chances.

"Come out to the deck in the rear, where you can have a better view." Norton invited with mock politeness.

Gun barrels of the guards prodded Johnny along.

"I want you to watch as your friends, one by one, go on their last long fall," Norton added. "Of course, they are already dead, but not even a magician could put them to-gether again after they drop five thousand feet, to land on trees or rocks."

Johnny shuddered. He could picture how those bodies would look. And while Monk, Ham and Renny appeared dead, Johnny remembered, or thought he did, that he also must have looked the same way once. But he was alive now.

"Later, much later, I'm going to drop you overside, also," Norton was promising. "Before I do, I'll explain several things to you. For when you go over, you will have no parachute attached. I'm not in the least afraid you will survive to talk."

Johnny's face got hard. He was not afraid of threats of that kind. In fact, he wasn't afraid of death—particularly if his friends were going to die. And so far as he knew, only one of them was still breathing besides himself.

Major Thomas J. Roberts, called "Long Tom," had not been along with Doc. Long Tom was the electrician of the group. The last Johnny had heard, Long Tom had been in Europe, studying a new electrical development there. Evi-dently he had not returned in time for this trip. It was just as well, Johnny thought bleakly. If Long Tom had been along, then Doc's entire band would have been wiped out.

They came out on the deck at the stern of the airship. Johnny darted a quick glance behind them, and whatever hope he might have had, died then. The cloud he had been watching was drifting behind rapidly. It was more than a mile to the rear already.

"I think," Sleek Norton was cogitating, "that we will push the ape overboard first, and watch through glasses to see what happens when his body lands. Then we can more properly appreciate it when the others go."

Chapter XIX

A DIRIGIBLE FALLS

JOHNNY might not have been so completely downhearted had he been able to watch the strange-appearing cloud all the time. Once for just a few brief minutes, it had overhauled the dirigible. In those few minutes, several things had happened.

The cloud had seemed to stick right on top of the dirigible. And under cover of that protective blankness, three forms had moved swiftly.

The first was the tall, bronze figure of Doc Savage. Next had come the tattered-clothed form of Scotty Falcorn. Last, and almost squealing in his delight, despite orders to the contrary, was Habeas Corpus.

A trapdoor opened right on top of the dirigible. Only Doc knew of that door, and of the small entranceway it made into the heart of the giant airship.

As soon as the three figures had disappeared, the cloud appeared to fade back. The cloud still covered the Autogiro Doc Savage had used to overhaul the dirigible. Doc had stopped the propeller in front, however, and only the giro blades now kept the craft aloft.

Doc Savage should have been killed; in fact, the Indian had been right in thinking he saw the bronze man go to his doom. But the Indian had been mistaken as well. Even while fleeing from the jungle cats at top speed, Doc worked swiftly.

First, he had taken an ointment from his emergency kit, which he had smeared on his head, face and body. That removed the blood odor from his person. Then he had taken off most of his clothes, and all of those that had the false odor on them.

When Doc had been just about to be overhauled, he had dropped the clothing. That was what the cats had seized

They had still been fighting over it when they went into the water.

At the moment the cats had sprung, Doc had dropped, seized a giant hanging vine. The force of his fall swung him far to one side. Safe in another tree, he had watched the cats go to their death

The bronze man had remained in concealment while the Indian had investigated He had wanted Sleek Norton to believe him dead.

Then he had really made time.

The giro Doc found undamaged in the field where he had first landed with Monk and Ham. Ham had turned off the power on the giro when he went overboard in his chute, but the giant blades had brought the craft down to a safe and easy landing,

Then Doc had sped toward Sleek Norton's hide-out. He had arrived there too late to prevent the racketeer from taking off. But shots were still roaring when the bronze man appeared

Habeas greeted him like a long-lost friend. A few moments later Doc slipped Scotty Falcorn from the hideout. With Scotty and Habeas, he sped back to the giro. The false cloud had been easy to create The chase and overhauling of the dirigible had followed

Now Doc led the way into the belly of the big ship. The passageway was just large enough to let his huge body through. The others trailed without difficulty

Doc stopped in a small room. The room was in the center of the helium bags that supported the ship Not even his aids knew of the existence of this secret place The bronze man moved to one wall, flicked a switch There was a low, purring noise. Scotty Falcorn exclaimed in surprise as one side of the room became luminous Dim objects could be seen Then those objects stood out in sharp relief. The entire wall was a big television receiving set. Almost every part of the ship was visible on that wall.

Doc's low, trilling sound filled the room. Without a second's hesitation, he tore through a doorway, into another part of the big bag. Plainly visible in one corner of the room was a picture of what was occurring on the stern of the ship Two gunmen, at Norton's orders, had swaggered forward They had picked up Chemistry's body and were walking toward the rail.

JOHNNY lunged forward ineffectively. He didn't know what he could do with his arms tied tightly, but he intended to try—even if it was nothing more than kick the two gunmen overboard when they tossed Chemistry's body over the side.

Norton languidly stretched out one foot. Johnny tripped, went to the floor.

"Get up!" Sleek snapped harshly. "I want you to see this. And don't try another act or I'll put a bullet in you, not where it will kill, but merely disable. It will hit you in some pleasant spot, like the kneecap."

Sweat was rolling from Johnny's face. He had to bite his lip to keep back hot words. But he remained silent. He did not intend to give Sleek Norton the pleasure of seeing him plead.

Gloria Delpane also had been brought to the stern deck. Her face was pale, but her eyes were almost unseeing. The shock of knowing that her brother had been left behind, of believing, in fact, that he might have been shot down right at the last, had left her numbed.

Hugo Parks chuckled as Sleek barked a sharp order. Again the two gunmen moved toward the rail. They lifted the ape's body high, prepared to throw it. And then a surprising thing happened.

The day was calm, the wind light. But the dirigible bucked suddenly, as if it had encountered a severe storm! The big airship rolled far over to one side. The rail toward which the gunmen had been walking was on the top side. The gunmen dropped Chemistry to the deck, rolled across until they hit the netting at the opposite side.

Johnny went off his feet. The girl hit the deck. Even Sleek Norton was tossed from the chair in which he had been sitting. An instant later, the dirigible righted itself.

Sleek Norton's face was a fiery red. Hugo Parks was cursing as he nursed several bruises. The gunmen, frightened, leaped to their feet. "Try it again," Norton bellowed. "We must have hit a down draft of wind or something. There's nothing to be afraid of."

The gunmen approached Chemistry's body cautiously. Gingerly, they picked him up, moved slowly toward the rail. Then they ran the last few steps, tried to throw the ape's body overboard.

For a second time the dirigible rolled. This time, it canted over even more sharply than before. And once again the gunmen went down. Chemistry's body fell safely on the deck.

Sleek Norton's face had lost its color. The first time might have been an accident; but when it happened twice in a row, the racketeer knew the actions of the dirigible were no accident. Someone or something was making it behave like that.

Norton almost dreaded to think of the only possible explanation that came to his mind. His voice was fierce as he roared the orders: "Search the ship! Search it from one end to the other! Shoot anything you see!"

Then he, himself, also grabbed a Tommy gun. With Hugo Parks at his heels, the racketeer led the search.

DOC SAVAGE'S gold-flecked eyes were flashing. He was in the lower section of the dirigible. About him were the gyroscopes he had installed to keep the dirigible on an even keel during rough weather.

Those gyroscopes, however, could be made to unsettle as well as settle the ship's sway. Through television sets, Doc could see just when to throw the ship off balance, to prevent Chemistry from being dropped five thousand feet to the ground below.

As Sleek Norton ordered a search of the ship, the bronze man abandoned his post. He made his way to his laboratory. Much of his valuable equipment had been lost or destroyed while he was in the jungle. He needed to replace it.

Above, in the secret room, Scotty Falcorn had been busy also. Scotty was like a man reborn. Doc Savage had removed him from the peril of instant death; had given him a chance for life. Falcorn was more than grateful. His eyes flashed joyfully as he found a sub-machine gun hidden in the room. Then he found a supply of ammunition. Some of that ammunition contained tracer bullets.

Scotty Falcorn no longer appeared inefficient. He was an

army-trained flier. He knew what to do with machine guns and tracer bullets, even though his mind was still dazed.

Scotty had undergone much. His ship had cracked up while he was trying a distance flight. Then he had been seized by the Indians. No matter what happened from now on, Scotty knew that experience would always be a nightmare to him. Only the calm, sure confidence of the bronze man had given him nerve enough to break away from the Indians.

Now he left the secret room, closing the door behind him and leaving Habeas Corpus there. But he did not follow Doc's course lower in the dirigible. He retraced his steps toward the top. Scotty Falcorn remembered that the gunners who had tried to kill him were in the second dirigible.

That dirigible had been a full mile away. But the strange twists and sweeps of Doc's airship had been seen. Radio messages brought no response. Norton was too busy searching the ship. So the men aboard the racketeer's dirigible began to draw closer. They wanted to find out what the trouble was.

The two bags were only a short distance apart when Scotty Falcorn put his head up cautiously from the opening in the top of the metal cigar. The flier's breath came in sharply. Slowly, he eased the machine gun over the top, looked through the sights. He should have been invisible. It was poor luck more than anything else that caused a gunman aboard the second ship to see Scotty's head.

The gunman could not make out who was behind the gun. He didn't care. It was enough for him that a gun was pointed his way. He grabbed a pistol, started to throw hot lead at Scotty's dimly-seen figure.

Scotty Falcorn smiled thinly and happily. He preferred to get the others in a fight, anyway. Then he pressed the trigger. A streak of flame shot out as the tracer bullets sped toward their target. Scotty painted his initials in the bag of the other dirigible. And Norton's ship had not been filled with helium. It contained the highly inflammable hydrogen.

There was a terrific blast and a sheet of flame. Doc's ship seemingly was hurled a half mile through the air, so violent was the concussion.

But of the other bag only flaming fragments remained. Scotty Falcorn had at least revenged the helpless Indians who had been shot down. All aboard the second ship were dead.

GUNMEN aboard Doc's dirigible came running from all sides. They gathered on the deck at the stern, faces incredulous. They had heard the firing of a submachine gun, but still they could not credit the swift destruction of their sister ship and the men who had been on it.

Johnny did not like to have men die, but he could see grim justice in their end. They had lived by fire, and they had died that way. And the tall, lean geologist was just as much mystified as the others as to who had fired the fatal shots.

Johnny had been slightly hopeful when the dirigible had gone through its stunts. Now he wasn't, for he knew Doc would never cause such loss of life—not if it could be prevented.

Hugo Parks was raging when he hit the deck. His large head was rocking from side to side. "Get to work! Search this ship!" he screeched at the open-mouthed gunmen.

The men hastened to obey. But at the last moment, Parks looked crafty. He stopped two of the men, told them to get in hiding, but to remain on the stern deck.

As Parks disappeared, the sleek, well-dressed form of Norton came into view. He carried two hypodermic needles in his hand. His lips were drawn back, hard.

The hidden gunmen half rose when they saw him, then relaxed again with grins. Norton was angry. They knew something amusing usually happened when the racketeer became thoroughly sore.

Johnny's heart sank. He could guess the reason for those two hypos, or, at least, he thought he could. Norton must be afraid that there was some cure for the green death. He was going to take no chances with his victims.

The dapper figure went first to the body of the ape. Chemistry's mummified form did not stir as a long needle bit into him, heading directly toward his heart. Then Norton turned his attention to Monk, Ham and Renny. To each in turn, he jabbed the long needle. It also went in their hearts.

Next the sleek figure turned. He had the second hypodermic in his hand as he walked directly to Johnny.

The lean geologist gasped, his eyes wide. "Well, I'll be superamalgamated!" he told himself.

The man Johnny watched was clad in the sartorially-perfect garments of Sleek Norton. His features appeared the same—but his eyes were the gold-flaked pools of Doc Savage.

The bronze man gave no sign of recognition as he bent over Johnny. If he spoke at all, his voice was too low to be heard by the watching guards. Then came a shout. There was a blur of motion. A second Sleek Norton, the real one, appeared at the door to the deck.

Behind him was Hugo Parks. Presence of the large-headed man explained why Norton had showed up. The sleek racketeer had been left tied and bound by Doc. But he had been discovered, only minutes later, by his aid.

Armed men were with them. In Norton's hand was a large lead box.

Scotty Falcorn chose that moment to fall onto the deck. He came from a trapdoor overhead. Scotty had been investigating, trying to find how to reach Doc, when he had found the trapdoor and heard voices underneath. He hadn't expected to make such a dramatic entry, but his feet had slipped. The sub-machine gun fell from his fist as he swatted the deck.

Sleek Norton grabbed Gloria Delpane, held her in front of him like a shield. "At last," he said, "I believe I have everyone just where I want them! You will all remain quiet, please."

There was that in his voice which made it seem well to obey.

Chapter XX

THE REAL GREEN DEATH

Doc Savage could have attacked; he might possibly have reached Sleek Norton without difficulty. But the gunmen would have opened fire. And more than Doc's life was at stake. He could not risk the life of Gloria Delpane, her brother, or that of Renny.

The bronze man stood quietly. "And now, Norton?" he asked softly. His face did not change expression.

Sleek Norton's features did. They became savage and wild. A killing light flared in his eyes. "You are smart, Doc Savage, very smart," he gloated. "But this time you have reached the end of the trail."

Doc Savage did not move. Hugo Parks also assumed a gloating expression.

"In this lead box I have the green death," Norton said. His gunmen stared, some started to draw back. Norton stopped them with a gesture. "I will tell you when to run," he snapped. He spoke again to the bronze man.

"As I know you have figured it out, Mr. Savage," he went on silkily, "the green death is caused by a plant growing in the Green Hell, a plant that resembles grass."

Doc remained quiet. His very stillness seemed to infuriate Sleek Norton.

"I will make a fortune with this grass," Norton shrieked, "for I know how to bring its victims back to life!"

Johnny's jaw dropped. Perhaps he hadn't been dreaming after all. Maybe he had died and been brought back to life.

Norton motioned the girl back. With her brother, she withdrew until she stood side by side with the bronze man. If Doc moved at all, Sleek Norton did not see him. Even if it seemed that the girl gave a faint gasp of pain, the racketeer did not notice. He was too busy explaining what he was going to do.

"This grass only works in the daytime, as you also know," Norton sneered. "At night, it is harmless; but when the sun shines it has almost instant effect.

"I intend to use it in the States. And there are many uses I can put it to. In kidnaping, for instance, the victim never even knows what happens to him. He stays on ice, figuratively speaking, until ransom is paid. Then an antidote is shot in him. He revives several hours later, but can tell nothing.

"Or I can use it for death insurance—and later bring my men back to life. Or again—and best of all—I can affect the wife of a rich man with the green death. He would pay anything for a remedy. And he would pay. If he didn't——"

Sleek Norton's eyes were hideous. Hugo Parks also was gloating. The gunmen had drawn back. The terrible things Norton planned were almost too much for them to stomach.

"I thought first I needed you," Norton went on. "The Indians told us that sometimes those who died of the green death came back as ghosts. I guessed there must be a remedy, and sent Parks for you. Then Pterlodin walked in of his own accord. He wanted us to help him become a king."

Sleek Norton laughed as though at a very amusing joke. "Pterlodin was the medicine man, the one man in all Matto Grosso who knew the answer I wanted. He gave it to me, and he gave me also the drugs to make myself immune. Both Parks and I have used that drug."

Behind Doc, Renny moved slightly. Monk and Ham also appeared to be of a lighter greenish shade. Norton saw— and laughed again.

"In this box I have a handful of green leaves," he said. "I am going to toss them on the deck. You will all be overcome. Before anything else can happen, you will be hurled to death."

His arm swung dramatically. His gunmen turned and fled. There would have been no time for Doc to act, even if he had so desired—and he did not seem to wish to move.

Norton's hand came out. A green shower fell on the deck about the feet of Doc, Gloria, Johnny and Scotty. The leaves were in the sun. A faint, sweetish odor filled the air.

Then a cry split the air. But the cry came from Sleek Norton. The racketeer was looking at his own hand. That hand had turned slightly green.

A shriek came from Hugo Parks. He also was beginning to change color. "The antidote!" yelled Parks.

He turned, dived into a cabin. Sleek Norton knocked him aside as they fought through the doorway. With frantic fingers, Norton grabbed a hypodermic.

"I KNOW I ain't in heaven," came Monk's wistful voice. "I see too many people I know around me."

"They don't let apes in heaven," Ham's voice came weakly.

"Nor lawyers, either, I expect," Renny's dry, severe tones added.

A sigh of relief came from Johnny. The lean geologist didn't know yet how it had all happened, or what the result would be. He didn't particularly care.

A yell came from Scotty Falcorn when the flier found he was still alive. He grabbed the submachine gun off the deck, raced in pursuit of the fleeing gunmen.

Then Doc moved. He moved rapidly. He raced to the room where Norton and Parks had gone. He had his own hypodermic in his hand.

The racketeer and his big-headed aid were stretched out on the floor. Their bodies were very green. They appeared as if they had been long dead. Norton still clutched a hypo. That hypo was driven into Parks's arm. Norton had jabbed it there after first taking a shot himself.

The bronze man kneeled beside them, inserted his own hypodermic. Then he withdrew it, and his low, trilling sound filled the cabin.

"Gone?" asked Johnny, beside him.

Doc Savage nodded slowly. "Pterlodin double-crossed them," he explained. "I was afraid of that. What they thought was an antidote, one that would bring them back to life, really brought their death. The tissues of their bodies have disintegrated. There is nothing I can do for them."

Monk and Ham, with Renny, were on their feet. Chemistry also had staggered up. They helped Scotty Falcorn round up the gunmen. That wasn't a difficult job. In only a few minutes the gangsters had been captured and locked into a large storeroom.

They would be taken back to New York. Before long,

they would visit Doc's upstate New York sanitarium, but they didn't know that.

"THE condition of the man's body in New York gave me the first clue," Doc explained some time later. "I found that every pore had been stopped."

"In other words, he was in a state of suspended animation, with all bodily functions stopped?" Renny asked.

The bronze man nodded. "That state could last indefinitely. I started to look for the cause and suspected the shirt. I think that was right. When we located the shirt on the dirigible, I found where something had been placed over the heart. That undoubtedly was a leaf, which Parks removed before the shirt came into Miss Delpane's possession."

"I suppose, because the leaf had wilted, that it worked somewhat slower?" Ham suggested.

"I believe so," Doc agreed. "Parks must have brought the leaves back concealed in the lead box he had."

"But the antidote?" Monk piped.

"While we were on the dirigible," Doc said, "I prepared a compound that partly counteracted the effects of the grass."

Monk nodded. They had all been given a shot of that, although none had known what it was at the time. That explained why they had recovered so rapidly.

"Later, when I had some of the grass in my possession, I was able to prepare a more complete cure and preventive," Doc said. His statement was calm. He was not boasting. The others knew he was not. The bronze man took it for granted that he should be able to do such things. He had trained for them all his life.

"I suppose it would be possible to partly recover, and then act subconsciously?" Johnny asked.

"I believe so," Doc nodded. "I think Pterlodin did that to you; and that while you were dazed, you wrote the note which we found. Pterlodin did not know what the note said, but he took it to Norton, and Norton realized the value."

"How about the two men in New York?" Renny asked.

For the first time, a faint flicker of expression crossed Doc's face. It was the slightest shade of a smile. "They are in good hands," he said. "I radioed instructions. I am sure they are alive—and in jail."

"Which only leaves our double-crossing friend—Pterlodin," Monk sighed. "I'd like to know what became of him."

PTERLODIN would have liked even Monk's company at that moment. The medicine man was seeing things he did not believe, things that could not be true, because he had not willed them that way.

The medicine man was not completely back in the good graces of Princess Molah. But he was a fast talker. He had saved his life. Now he was near the entrance to the cavern of the dead. The next moment, he wasn't. He was far from there.

The door to the cavern opened. Figures started to emerge, figures that should have been dead. A majority of the green death victims who were in the burial vault were there because they had displeased the medicine man. He had been forced to work slowly and craftily, but it had been noticed that those who opposed him too much, died.

He had been permitted to get away with plenty. The secret of the green death was one that had been handed down from medicine man to medicine man each generation. None other was allowed to know it.

Pterlodin even had grinned to himself when Norton belived he was getting the real antidote and the correct preventive serum.

The tribe itself had concurred in having one person know the secret. The grass had been developed through centuries of work. It guarded the only vulnerable entrance to the cliff city. The fewer who knew that it was inactive at night, and that its effect could be counteracted, the better.

Pterlodin first thought he was seeing ghosts. Then he knew that he wasn't. The bronze man had been even a greater medicine man than he had supposed. He had given each victim a shot before leaving the cavern of the dead.

The shot had not been as powerful as that given Johnny. Doc had not wanted the women there to revive too quickly. But they had recovered now.

Pterlodin would have cried out if he had thought it would help him, but he knew that it would not. So he trusted to the speed of his short legs. Behind him, the revived victims of his deadliness set up a shouting. They took after him as fast as they could.

It was Zehi who saw the reanimated squadron of the death first—saw them and the running medicine man. Zehi had been daydreaming, she had been thinking of the bronze man, and regretting that he was gone, even though she knew it had been necessary for him to leave.

She stood directly beneath one of the more ornate paintings, one ornamented with many colored stones. Those stones were emeralds, each one worth a fortune. Zehi did not know that. Only Doc Savage had noticed them; had realized their value. And Doc Savage would never tell.

Zehi grabbed a spear. She sent out a warning cry. Soon a half-hundred amazons were after Pterlodin. They also had seen and understood that those who had appeared dead were no longer dead, and that Pterlodin himself should die.

The end came quite suddenly. The medicine man ran too close to the sacred fire. He did not see Princess Molah until he was almost upon her. Then it was too late.

The spear in Princess Molah's hand jabbed out. Pterlodin dodged to avoid it. He stepped into the pit of fire. He had time for only one agonized yell before the end came.

ALL was peaceful on the dirigible. The Matto Grosso section was rapidly being left behind. And those aboard the airship were trying to forget their experiences in the jungle.

At dusk, Monk strolled to the rear deck of the dirigible. Doc was up ahead, working again in his laboratory. The bronze man always worked, it seemed to Monk. The chemist had other affairs at hand. He caught sight of a figure seated in a chair near the stern rail.

Monk glanced about hastily and a little guiltily. He breathed a sigh of relief when he saw no one else near by. Then he tiptoed forward and dropped into an adjoining chair.

"G-Gloria," he said. His piping voice had an unusual tremor.

The figure, cloaked against the cool air of dusk, did not move.

Monk sighed, got up his courage. Slowly, cautiously, he put out one arm, pressed it about the figure next to him.

Then he pulled that figure toward him, his lips opened and closing in delicious anticipation.

The figure turned suddenly. Monk found himself staring into the hairy face of Chemistry. Lights flashed on. A flashlight boomed. Ham stood grinning, a camera in his hand.

Monk was a brave man. He had proved that often. But just this one time he wished that Doc had not been quite so quick to bring him back to life. It took no seer to imagine what Ham intended to do with that picture.

But Monk was game. He turned Chemistry's head on around, brought his lips close.

"At least, you can't kid me about it, dang it!" he said.